Forever
in a
Moment

Abhinav Jain

AF121028

NewDelhi • London

BLUEROSE PUBLISHERS
India | U.K.

Copyright © Abhinav Jain 2025

All rights reserved by author. No part of this publication may be reproduced, stored in a retrieval system or transmitted in any form or by any means, electronic, mechanical, photocopying, recording or otherwise, without the prior permission of the author. Although every precaution has been taken to verify the accuracy of the information contained herein, the publisher assumes no responsibility for any errors or omissions. No liability is assumed for damages that may result from the use of information contained within.

BlueRose Publishers takes no responsibility for any damages, losses, or liabilities that may arise from the use or misuse of the information, products, or services provided in this publication.

For permissions requests or inquiries regarding this publication, please contact:

BLUEROSE PUBLISHERS
www.BlueRoseONE.com
info@bluerosepublishers.com
+91 8882 898 898
+4407342408967

ISBN: 978-93-7018-172-4

Cover Design: Aman Sharma
Typesetting: Pooja Sharma

First Edition: May 2025

Dedication

To my beloved wife, Ritu

Your love, patience, and unwavering support have been the foundation of my journey. Through every late night, every moment of doubt, and every page written, you stood beside me, believing in me even when I struggled to believe in myself.

This book is not just a creation of words, but a reflection of your encouragement, your kindness, and the inspiration you bring into my life every day. Thank you for being my greatest source of strength and my forever muse.

With all my love,

Abhinav

Preface

Arjun, a reserved novelist battling writer's block, has spent years lost in the stories he creates, avoiding the unpredictability of real life. But when he crosses paths with Natasha, a free-spirited artist who paints her emotions onto every canvas, his world shifts in ways he never imagined.

Their love is quiet yet intense—an unspoken promise that neither of them can deny. But Natasha carries a past she has never shared, one that threatens to pull them apart just as they find their way to each other. As old wounds resurface and time works against them, Arjun and Natasha must fight their fears, their pasts, and fate itself to hold onto a love that feels like destiny.

About Author

Abhinav Jain is a corporate professional working with one of the AI startups in Gurgaon as a Recruitment Leader. He is an author renowned for his contributions to recruitment practices and literature, particularly in the genres of fantasy and inspirational fiction, and is fond of writing poems and ghazals. Born and raised in Uttar Pradesh, Abhinav's early life in this culturally rich region has significantly influenced his storytelling, infusing his narratives with depth and authenticity.

Abhinav pursued higher education at XLRI, where he earned a Postgraduate Certificate in Human Resource Management (PGCHRM) and a Bachelor of Technology (B.Tech.) from IASE University, Rajasthan.

Beyond his professional and literary endeavors, Abhinav is a man of diverse interests. He harbors a deep appreciation for soft music. His artistic inclinations extend to writing poems and ghazals, allowing him to express creativity. An avid reader, Abhinav believes in the transformative power of literature, considering words to be a form of magic that can inspire and enlighten.

Abhinav advocates for the exploration and sharing of one's inherent talents. He posits that individuals should endeavor to uncover and showcase their hidden abilities, as withholding them would deprive the world of potential beauty and innovation. This belief underscores his own journey as a writer and educator, continually striving to contribute positively to society.

Abhinav maintains an active presence on social media platforms, particularly LinkedIn and Instagram, where he connects with readers and shares insights into his creative process.

Chapter 1:
The Blank Page

The cursor blinked on the empty screen, taunting him like an unanswered question.

Arjun Mehra exhaled, rubbing his temples as he stared at the glowing white void on his laptop. The quiet hum of the air conditioner and the occasional honk of a distant car were the only sounds in his dimly lit apartment. He had been sitting like this for hours, his fingers hovering over the keyboard, waiting for the words to come. But they didn't. They hadn't for weeks.

He reached for his coffee mug, only to realize it had gone cold. He frowned, glancing at the time on the bottom corner of his screen— **11:47 PM**.

With a frustrated sigh, he shut the laptop and leaned back in his chair, staring at the ceiling. The walls of his study were lined with bookshelves, each filled with novels that had once inspired him. His own books sat among them, their glossy covers reflecting the soft light from the desk lamp. He should have felt proud looking at them. Instead, they were a reminder of something he was slowly losing—his ability to write.

Arjun had never believed in writer's block. He had always been the kind of writer who could lose himself in his stories, effortlessly weaving together characters and emotions. But now, the words felt foreign, just out of reach. His last novel had been a bestseller, praised for its depth and emotion, but now, the pressure to deliver something equally powerful weighed on him like a stone.

Maybe he had nothing left to say.

The thought sent a flicker of unease through him, and he abruptly pushed back his chair. He needed air.

Grabbing his jacket, he stepped out of his apartment and onto the streets of Mumbai. The city was still alive, even at this hour. Street vendors packed up their stalls, couples walked hand in hand under the dim glow of streetlights, and the distant sound of a saxophone filled the air with a melancholic tune.

Arjun walked without a destination, letting the rhythm of the city guide him. He had always found solace in the quiet chaos of Mumbai—the way life never truly stopped, the way every street held a different story. And yet, tonight, even the city felt distant, like he was walking through a memory rather than reality.

That was when he saw it.

A small art gallery stood at the corner of the street, its warm light spilling onto the pavement. A sign above the door read:

"Brush Strokes—One Night Only"

Something about the name tugged at him, an odd sense of familiarity he couldn't place. Before he could second-guess himself, he pushed open the glass door and stepped inside.

The scent of oil paint and fresh canvas filled the air, mingling with the faint notes of jazz playing from a vintage record player in the corner.

The gallery was small, intimate, the walls adorned with paintings that spoke in colors rather than words.

Arjun wandered through the space, his gaze moving from one canvas to the next. Some paintings were abstract, a blur of emotions captured in brushstrokes. Others were hauntingly detailed—portraits of people who seemed to be caught in unspoken moments, their eyes telling stories their lips never could.

And then he saw it.

A painting that stopped him in his tracks.

It was a whirlwind of colors—deep blues clashing with fiery reds, soft yellows melting into streaks of violet. There was something chaotic about it, yet it felt strangely comforting, like watching a storm rage from behind a window. It was raw, unfiltered emotion splashed across a canvas.

It felt… familiar.

A voice pulled him from his thoughts.

"Do you like it?"

He turned.

Standing beside him was a woman, her arms crossed, a smirk playing on her lips. She was different from the polished gallery visitors around them—her white shirt was splattered with paint, her dark, wavy hair tied up in a loose bun, stray strands falling around her face. Her eyes—deep brown with flecks of gold—held a spark of mischief, as if she already knew the answer to the question she had just asked.

Arjun hesitated. "It's… intense."

She chuckled. "That's an artist's way of saying you don't understand it."

A small smirk tugged at his lips. "No, I do. It feels like—" He searched for the right words. "Like someone trying to say something but not knowing how."

For the first time, her teasing expression softened.

"Maybe that's exactly what it is."

There was a pause, a moment where they simply stood there, looking at the painting as if it held the answer to something neither of them had asked out loud.

Arjun shifted, suddenly curious. "Who painted this?"

She grinned. "I did."

He blinked. "You?"

"Disappointed?" she teased.

He glanced at the painting again. Now that he knew, it made sense. There was something in the way she carried herself—unapologetic yet reserved, bold yet unreadable—that matched the energy of the artwork.

"No," he admitted. "Just surprised."

"Good," she said, tucking her hands into her pockets. "I like surprising people."

Something about her intrigued him. There was an effortless confidence in her, an air of unpredictability that he wasn't used to.

"You have a name?" he asked.

She tilted her head. "Natasha."

He nodded. "Arjun."

Her eyes narrowed slightly. "Arjun... as in Arjun Mehra, the novelist?"

He sighed. "Unfortunately, yes."

Her laughter was light, unrestrained. "Why 'unfortunately'? People love your books."

"I think people love the idea of my books more than the books themselves," he said honestly.

Natasha studied him for a moment, as if trying to read between the lines. "Spoken like a writer who hasn't written in a while."

He gave her a wry look. "Is it that obvious?"

She shrugged. "You looked at this painting like it was saying something you've been trying to put into words."

Arjun glanced at the artwork again. Maybe she was right. Maybe that was why it had pulled him in—because it reminded him of the words he couldn't write.

Natasha leaned against the wall, her gaze flickering between him and the painting. Then, she smirked again. "Since you understand it so well, tell me—what do you think happens next?"

He frowned. "What do you mean?"

She gestured toward the painting. "If this were a story, what would the next chapter look like?"

Arjun studied the canvas, the way the colors swirled unpredictably, never settling, always in motion.

"I don't know," he admitted. "But I think I'd like to find out."

Her smile widened, something unreadable flickering in her eyes.

"Good," she said softly. "Because that's the best part of any story, isn't it? The not knowing."

And just like that, the night shifted.

He had walked into the gallery searching for inspiration, expecting nothing but another failed attempt to outrun his own thoughts. Instead, he had found a painting that spoke in the language he had forgotten, and an artist who seemed to understand something about him that he hadn't yet understood himself.

For the first time in a long time, Arjun felt like he wasn't just existing.

He was part of a story again.

And maybe, just maybe, it was only the beginning.

Chapter 2:
Colors of the Night

The gallery hummed with quiet conversations, but for Arjun, the world had shrunk to the space between him and Natasha. She stood with an easy confidence, her paint-stained fingers wrapped around a cup of hot coffee, watching him with an amused glint in her eyes. The air smelled of oil paints and aged wood, a faint hint of something old yet timeless, like the very essence of creativity that lingered in the room.

"So, tell me, Arjun Mehra," she said, swirling her coffee, "What brings a brooding writer to an art gallery on a random night?"

Arjun exhaled, glancing around the room as if searching for an answer within the paintings themselves. "Writer's block."

Natasha raised an eyebrow, a knowing smile playing on her lips. "Ah. The infamous creative drought. Sounds painful."

"It is."

She studied him for a moment, then leaned against the wall, her posture relaxed yet piercingly observant. "You know, people always say writer's block happens because you've run out of words. But I think it happens when you're afraid of the words you need to write."

Arjun tilted his head, intrigued. "And what do you think an artist's block is?"

Natasha took a slow sip of her coffee, her eyes never leaving his. "When you're afraid to feel what you need to paint."

He wasn't sure why, but her words struck something deep within him. Maybe because they sounded too much like the truth he had been avoiding. He had spent months staring at blank pages, not because he had nothing to say, but because he wasn't sure if he could face what needed to be written.

Natasha suddenly pushed off the wall, energy crackling around her. "Come on."

Arjun blinked. "Where?"

"Just trust me."

Before he could protest, she grabbed his wrist and led him through the back entrance of the gallery. They stepped into the night air, the scent of rain lingering in the streets, mixing with the distant aroma of fresh bread from a bakery closing for the night. The city pulsed with life, neon lights flickering, horns blaring, and people lost in their own little worlds. But Natasha moved through it like she belonged to another world entirely—one where colors spoke louder than words and emotions bled onto canvases instead of staying trapped inside.

They walked for several minutes until they reached a narrow alleyway filled with street art—walls covered in layers of stories told in bold strokes of color. It was beautiful in a way that felt raw, untamed. Natasha stopped in front of a half-finished mural, a mix of blues and golds that seemed to dance in the dim light.

"This is where I come when I feel stuck," she said, pulling out a small can of spray paint from her bag.

Arjun watched as she shook the can and pressed it against the wall, adding a swirl of red to the painting. There was no hesitation, no overthinking—just pure instinct. She turned to him and held out the can.

"Your turn."

He frowned. "I don't paint."

"So?" She shrugged. "This isn't about being good. It's about letting go."

Arjun hesitated, then took the can. The cold metal felt unfamiliar in his hand. He stepped closer to the wall, the scent of paint filling his lungs, pressing down. A streak of deep green cut across the mural. It wasn't perfect. It wasn't even intentional. But somehow, it felt... freeing.

Natasha grinned. "See? You just created something."

He turned to her, something shifting inside him. "Yeah. I guess I did."

Their eyes met, and for the first time in a long time, Arjun felt something stir within him—not just inspiration, but possibility.

Natasha stepped back, admiring their work. "Every story starts with a single mark. Maybe this is yours."

Arjun wasn't sure if she was talking about the painting or something much bigger. But for the first time in months, he felt like he was on the verge of writing again.

And maybe, just maybe, this was where his real story began.

They stood there for a while, the cool night air wrapping around them, the hum of the city distant yet present. Natasha leaned against the wall, her fingers tracing an invisible pattern in the air. "Tell me, Arjun," she mused, "What's the story you're afraid to write?"

He swallowed, the weight of her question settling deep in his chest. "One that matters too much," he admitted. "One that might change everything."

Her eyes flickered with understanding. "Then that's the one you have to write."

Silence stretched between them, filled with unspoken thoughts and unfinished dreams. The city pulsed, lights flickering like a heartbeat, as if urging them forward. And in that moment, standing in an alleyway filled with color and chaos, Arjun knew that something had shifted—within him and between them. This was more than just a chance encounter. This was the start of something neither of them could yet define.

Natasha tossed him another can of spray paint, the corner of her lips curling into a challenge. "Think you're up for another mark?"

Arjun smirked, shaking the can. "I think I just might be."

As the night stretched on, the two of them painted, talked, and lost themselves in the simple act of creating. And somewhere between the streaks of paint and the spaces between their words, Arjun felt the first real tug of inspiration he had known in years.

Perhaps the story he was meant to write wasn't just on paper. Perhaps it had already begun—here, in the quiet defiance of an alleyway, in the laughter of a woman who saw the world in colors, and in the writer who had almost forgotten how to see at all.

Chapter 3:
Unfinished Canvases

The scent of spray paint lingered in the air as Arjun and Natasha stepped back to admire their impromptu creation. The wall before them was a chaotic mix of colors—wild, imperfect, yet strangely captivating. Streaks of red bled into deep blues, gold intertwining with green, creating a piece that neither of them could have planned but both seemed to understand instinctively.

Natasha grinned, tilting her head as she took in their work. "Not bad for your first time, Writer."

Arjun smirked, shaking the last few drops of paint from the can. "I think I'll stick to words."

She turned to face him, her dark eyes glinting under the flickering streetlight. "Maybe words aren't enough for what you want to say."

Her comment lingered in the space between them, heavy with meaning. Arjun wanted to ask what she meant, but something about Natasha told him she preferred mysteries left unsolved. She seemed like the kind of person who lived in the in-betweens, who thrived in uncertainty, where life was messy and art didn't need to be contained.

The streets were quieter now, the city slowly winding down for the night. They walked side by side, their pace unhurried, their footsteps echoing softly against the pavement. The air was thick with the scent of rain, the promise of an impending downpour hanging in the sky.

"So," Natasha said, breaking the silence, "what kind of stories do you write?"

Arjun exhaled, running a hand through his hair. "Love stories. But not the grand, dramatic kind. The quiet ones. The ones that happen in stolen moments, between people who don't realize they're falling until it's too late."

She smiled softly. "Like this moment?"

He glanced at her, surprised by the question. The way she looked at him—steady, curious, a little amused—made him feel as if he were already a character in one of his own stories. "Maybe."

Natasha didn't push for more. Instead, she led him to a small roadside tea stall nestled in a quiet corner of the city. The vendor, an elderly man with a kind face, poured steaming masala chai into clay cups, the rich aroma of spices filling the night air. Natasha handed Arjun a cup before taking one for herself, the warmth seeping into her fingers.

As they sat on a nearby bench, Natasha wrapped her fingers around her cup, staring at the city lights flickering in the distance. "You know, I used to believe that love should be like a painting—bold, messy, and full of passion."

Arjun took a slow sip of his tea, the warmth settling in his chest. "And now?"

She hesitated; her gaze distant. "Now I think love is more like an unfinished canvas. Sometimes, no matter how much you try to complete it, some parts remain untouched."

Her words held a weight that Arjun couldn't ignore. He wanted to ask about the parts of her life she had left unfinished, the stories she hadn't painted. But he sensed that Natasha wasn't ready to share just yet.

Instead, he said, "Maybe unfinished things are the most beautiful."

Natasha looked at him then, her eyes searching his, as if trying to decide whether she believed that. A breeze swept through the streets, carrying with it the quiet hum of the city. Neither of them spoke, but in that silence, something unspoken passed between them.

Maybe, Arjun thought, this was how love stories truly began—not in grand declarations, but in quiet, fleeting moments that lingered long after they were gone.

The rain arrived in soft drizzles, tapping against the pavement as Arjun and Natasha made their way through the winding streets. They weren't in a hurry. The night stretched out before them; the kind that made time feel like an illusion.

"So, why do you have writer's block?" Natasha asked suddenly, kicking a loose pebble on the ground.

Arjun sighed. He wasn't used to talking about it. "It's not that I don't have ideas. It's that I don't know if I want to write them."

She frowned, glancing at him. "Why not?"

"Because the words feel... too real. Too close." He hesitated, rubbing a hand over the back of his neck. "There's a story I've been avoiding. One I'm not sure I'm ready to tell."

Natasha nodded slowly, as if she understood. "Maybe that's the one you need to write."

He let out a soft chuckle. "You sound suspiciously like my old professor."

She smirked. "Well, your professor was probably right."

They stopped at an empty park, the swings swaying gently in the wind. Natasha sat on one, pulling her knees up as she rocked back and forth. "You know, art and writing aren't that different."

Arjun leaned against the swing set, watching her. "How so?"

She shrugged. "They both require you to face yourself. To be honest, even when it hurts."

He thought about that. Maybe that was the problem. Maybe he wasn't ready to face himself in the words he had to write.

The rain picked up slightly, droplets clinging to Natasha's dark curls. She didn't seem to mind. She tilted her head back, letting the coolness wash over her.

"Do you ever wish you could freeze a moment?" she asked suddenly.

Arjun studied her—the way the streetlights cast a golden glow on her face, the way the rain glistened on her skin. "Yeah," he admitted. "All the time."

Natasha gave him a small, knowing smile. "Then maybe that's your story."

They sat there for a while, the city moving around them, time slipping through their fingers. Arjun wasn't sure what this night meant, or if it even needed to mean anything. But for the first time in a long time, he felt something stir inside him—something like inspiration, something like hope.

And maybe, just maybe, that was enough to begin again.

Chapter 4:
A Story Waiting to Be Told

The next morning, Arjun sat at his desk, fingers hovering over his laptop keyboard. The blinking cursor was still there, waiting. But for the first time in months, it didn't feel like an enemy.

His mind kept replaying the events of the night before—Natasha's laughter, the way her fingers moved so effortlessly with a paintbrush, the way her eyes darkened for just a second when she spoke of unfinished things. There was something about her—about the way she seemed so fearless in the face of uncertainty—that had stayed with him long after they had parted ways.

Without thinking, he typed:

"She walked like a brushstroke on an unfinished canvas—wild, unrestrained, yet careful not to let the colors bleed too much."

Arjun stopped, staring at the words. He exhaled. It wasn't much, but it was something.

A knock at his door pulled him from his thoughts. He wasn't expecting anyone.

When he opened it, Natasha stood there, a smirk on her lips, a takeaway coffee cup in her hand.

"Morning, writer," she said, handing him the cup.

Arjun raised an eyebrow. "How do you know where I live?"

Natasha shrugged. "I asked around. Mumbai's not as big as you think."

He chuckled, stepping aside to let her in. Natasha walked in like she belonged there, her eyes scanning the bookshelf, the scattered pages on his desk.

"So," she said, leaning against the window, "did you write?"

Arjun hesitated, then nodded. "A little."

Natasha grinned. "Good. Then you owe me a favor."

He narrowed his eyes. "That's not how this works."

"Sure it is," she said, taking a sip of her coffee. "I helped you break your writer's block. Now you help me."

Arjun crossed his arms. "With what?"

Natasha set her cup down and looked at him, something unreadable in her eyes. "Come with me. There's something I want to show you."

Fifteen minutes later, they were walking through a quiet neighborhood in Bandra. The streets were lined with old colonial houses, their walls covered in vines and faded paint. The air smelled of rain, the sky still heavy with the remnants of the last night's downpour. Natasha led him to one of the houses—a two-story home with a large, overgrown garden. The windows were covered in dust, the walls peeling, but there was something undeniably beautiful about it.

"This was my childhood home," she said softly.

Arjun glanced at her. "You grew up here?"

Natasha nodded. "Until I left."

There was something about the way she said it—like she had run away, not just moved.

She pushed open the rusted gate and stepped inside. The house was abandoned, but it still held echoes of a past life. A broken swing hung from a tree in the backyard. Old paintings were stacked against a wall, covered in dust and time. The scent of oil paint still lingered faintly, as if the walls themselves had absorbed years of creativity and refused to let them go.

Arjun watched as Natasha ran her fingers over one of the paintings— a half-finished portrait of a woman's face, the brushstrokes frozen mid-motion.

"My mother was an artist," she murmured. "She never finished this painting."

Arjun stayed quiet, sensing that this was a moment she had never shared with anyone before.

"She used to tell me," Natasha continued, "That paintings are like people. Some are meant to be complete, and some... are beautiful even when they're not."

She turned to face him then, a small, sad smile on her lips. "I think I'm one of those unfinished ones."

Arjun took a step closer, his voice quiet. "Maybe you're not unfinished. Maybe you're just waiting for the right colors."

Natasha looked at him for a long moment, and in her eyes, Arjun saw something shift—like she was letting him see a part of her that she had kept hidden for too long.

Then she exhaled, breaking the moment with a laugh. "Come on, writer. If you're going to write a love story, you need to live one first."

She grabbed his hand and pulled him toward the door.

Arjun didn't know where this story was going. But for the first time in years, he wasn't afraid to find out.

They spent the rest of the day wandering through the city, Natasha leading the way as if she had a map etched in her mind. They stopped at a tiny bookstore tucked between two cafes, where she insisted, he pick a random book and read the first sentence aloud.

"First lines are important," she said. "They set the tone for everything that comes after."

Arjun opened a book at random and read, "It was the best of times, it was the worst of times.'"

Natasha rolled her eyes. "Too famous. Try again."

He picked another and read, "The sky was the color of television, tuned to a dead channel.'"

She grinned. "Now that's a first line."

Later, they sat by the sea, watching the waves crash against the rocks. Natasha tossed pebbles into the water, her movements slow and thoughtful.

"You ever think about what it means to leave a mark?" she asked.

Arjun leaned back on his elbows. "You mean, like a legacy?"

She nodded. "Yeah. Like, do we write, do we paint, because we want to be remembered? Or do we do it because we have to?"

Arjun thought about it. "Maybe both."

She didn't say anything for a while. Then, finally, she murmured, "My mother always said that artists don't belong to themselves. Their work is always bigger than they are."

Arjun turned to look at her. "Do you believe that?"

She hesitated. "I don't know. But sometimes, I think she poured so much of herself into her art that there was nothing left for her."

Arjun didn't know how to respond to that. Instead, he reached for a pebble and tossed it into the water alongside hers.

As the sun began to set, they found themselves back at the abandoned house. Natasha stood at the entrance, looking up at it as if seeing it for the first time.

"Do you ever think about coming back?" Arjun asked quietly.

She shook her head. "Some places don't belong to you anymore."

Arjun wanted to tell her that wasn't true. That she could reclaim this space, this part of herself. But he also knew that some ghosts were too heavy to chase away with words.

Instead, he said, "Then maybe you should finish the painting."

Natasha turned to him, her eyes searching his. "Why?"

"Because unfinished things can still be beautiful," he said. "But sometimes, they deserve to be completed."

For the first time since they met, Natasha didn't have a quick comeback. She just stood there, the weight of his words settling around them.

And in that moment, Arjun knew—this wasn't just a story. This was something real. Something neither of them could walk away from now.

Chapter 5:
Tides of the Past

The wind carried the scent of nostalgia as Arjun and Natasha stepped out of the abandoned house. The weight of memories clung to the air, but Natasha walked ahead as if she could outrun them. Arjun followed, silent, giving her space to process whatever emotions the visit had stirred.

They walked in comfortable silence until they reached a quiet stretch of the beach. The city buzzed behind them, but here, under the open sky, the world felt smaller, more intimate.

Natasha sat on the cool sand, hugging her knees to her chest. Arjun settled beside her, waiting. He had learned by now that she would speak when she was ready.

"My mother used to paint here," she finally said, her voice barely above a whisper. "She believed the ocean could wash away anything. Pain. Regret. Even love."

Arjun glanced at her, but she was staring at the waves, lost in thought.

"What happened to her?" He asked gently.

Natasha hesitated, then exhaled. "She left."

The words were simple, but they carried the weight of something heavier.

"She walked out one evening and never came back," Natasha continued. "No goodbye. No explanation. Just gone."

Arjun's fingers curled into the sand. "You never found out why?"

She shook her head. "For years, I convinced myself she had a good reason. That she'd come back. But she didn't. And I realized—some people don't leave because they don't love you. They leave because they don't know how to stay."

Arjun watched her, his heart aching for the girl she had been—the one who had waited for someone who never returned.

"You don't have to be like her," he said softly.

Natasha turned to him, something raw flickering in her eyes. "But what if I already am? What if I don't know how to stay either?"

Arjun studied her, then reached down and picked up a seashell, pressing it into her palm.

"Then don't stay," he said. "But take something with you."

She looked down at the shell, running her fingers over its ridges. "And what about you?"

He smiled slightly. "I'll write the story, whether you stay or not."

Natasha let out a small, shaky laugh. "That's unfair. You always get to keep something."

Arjun shrugged. "That's the thing about writers—we turn everything into stories. Even the people we lose."

She stared at him for a moment, then shook her head with a smirk. "You're dangerous, Arjun Mehra."

He chuckled. "Why?"

"Because you make me want to believe in things I stopped believing in a long time ago."

The waves rolled in, erasing their footprints in the sand. But some things, Arjun knew, were impossible to erase.

Like the feeling of Natasha beside him.

Like the story they were writing together, one moment at a time.

The moon had risen by the time they left the beach, casting a silver glow over the quiet streets. They walked slowly, their shoulders almost touching, wrapped in a silence that felt like understanding rather than absence.

"I don't think I ever told anyone that," Natasha admitted as they neared her apartment. "About my mother."

Arjun glanced at her. "Why me?"

She gave him a lopsided smile. "Maybe because you won't try to fix it."

He nodded. "Some things aren't meant to be fixed."

"Yeah," she said softly. "Some things just need to be understood."

They reached her building, and for a moment, neither of them moved. Natasha looked up at her window, then back at him. "Do you want to come up?"

Arjun hesitated, not because he didn't want to, but because something about this moment felt fragile, like it could be broken if they weren't careful.

"Not tonight," he said finally. "But soon."

She nodded, seeming to understand. "Goodnight, writer."

"Goodnight, artist."

As she disappeared inside, Arjun stood there for a moment longer, the sea breeze still clinging to his skin, the taste of her words lingering in his mind.

And for the first time in a long time, he wasn't afraid of the story waiting to be written.

Chapter 6:
Unfinished Conversations

One evening, as they sat on the rooftop of Natasha's studio, watching the city lights flicker below, Arjun finally voiced the question that had been forming in the silence between them.

"What are you afraid of?"

Natasha, who had been sketching absentmindedly in her notebook, froze.

She looked up, meeting his gaze. "What do you mean?"

He leaned forward, resting his elbows on his knees. "You hold back. I see it. You pull away just when it feels like something real is happening."

Natasha closed her sketchbook, exhaling shakily. "Arjun…"

"Tell me," he said gently. "Let me understand."

She hesitated, then placed the sketchbook between them. "Do you want to see something?"

He picked it up and flipped through the pages.

Sketch after sketch, it was him—his profile as he wrote, the way he sipped his coffee, the curve of his smile when he thought no one was looking. Each one captured something real, something unguarded. Some of them were drawn with such depth that he felt as though they reflected not just his face but his very essence.

Arjun's throat tightened. "You've been drawing me?"

Natasha gave him a small, almost shy smile. "For weeks."

He looked at her, waiting.

She sighed, hugging her knees. "Do you know what the problem with art is?"

Arjun shook his head.

"You can pour your whole soul into it, but once it's out in the world, it's no longer yours." She paused, her voice barely above a whisper. "I think that's why I'm afraid of love. Because once you give someone your heart, it's no longer just yours."

Arjun stared at her, something deep inside him stirring. He understood that fear more than she realized. Love had cost him before. He knew the agony of giving someone your heart and watching them shatter it without a second thought.

"I get it," he said quietly. "Loving someone means giving them the power to hurt you."

Natasha looked at him, surprised. "Exactly."

He reached for the sketchbook, flipping to a blank page. Then, with slow, deliberate strokes, he wrote something.

When he turned the book back to her, she saw his words written in neat, careful handwriting:

"Not everything that is given is lost."

Natasha traced the words with her fingertips, as if trying to memorize them.

Arjun watched her, his voice softer now. "You don't have to be afraid, Natasha. Love doesn't mean losing yourself."

She didn't say anything for a long time. But then, she reached for his hand, lacing her fingers through his.

And for the first time, she didn't pull away.

But there was something in her eyes—something that lingered even as she let him in. A ghost of a memory, something buried deep within her.

But the moment didn't last. The next morning, Arjun found Natasha's studio door locked. The usual scent of coffee and paint lingering in the air was missing. She wasn't there.

A single note was taped to the door.

"I need time. Please don't look for me."

His heart sank. He had seen it coming—the flicker of fear in her eyes, the hesitation in her touch. But he had hoped, just this once that she wouldn't run.

As he stood there, uncertain of what to do, a gust of wind knocked something over near the doorway. It was her sketchbook, partially buried beneath scattered charcoal pencils. He hesitated before picking it up.

Flipping through the pages, he saw the familiar sketches of himself, but as he turned further, the images changed. They became darker, almost frantic. Scenes of a woman crying, running. A man in shadows. A storm outside a window.

The last page held only a single phrase, written in her delicate script.

"Some things aren't meant to be found."

A chill ran down his spine.

Who was Natasha running from?

And what was she afraid he would find?

His pulse quickened as he noticed something else. On the very last page, faintly imprinted beneath the words, was an address. The ink was smudged, as though she had written it in a hurry and then tried to erase it.

A place he didn't recognize.

Arjun clenched his jaw. His instincts screamed that this was more than just fear of commitment. This was something bigger. Something dangerous.

He closed his eyes, inhaling deeply, trying to piece together everything she had left unsaid. The Natasha he had come to know wasn't just an artist who loved quietly—she was someone hiding something, protecting herself from something in her past.

Was it heartbreak? Or something worse?

Arjun's hands clenched around the edges of the sketchbook. He couldn't let her disappear. Not without understanding the truth.

Because, deep down, he knew—whatever she was running from, it wasn't just the past. It was coming for her again.

Chapter 7:
The Ghosts We Bury

The address in Natasha's sketchbook burned in Arjun's mind. He wasn't sure whether she had meant for him to find it or if it was a mistake, a slip of the hand as she tried to erase it from existence. Either way, it was the only clue he had.

The streets were quiet as he walked through an unfamiliar neighborhood. The address led him to an old bookstore, tucked between abandoned buildings. Its wooden sign creaked in the wind, faded lettering barely legible—**Silver Pages.**

Pushing the door open, he stepped inside, the scent of aged paper and dust filling his lungs. The shop was dimly lit, lined with towering shelves that felt more like walls of memories than mere storage for books. The atmosphere was heavy, almost suffocating, as if the space itself held secrets that refused to be spoken aloud.

A woman behind the counter looked up, her expression shifting from curiosity to recognition. "You're looking for her, aren't you?"

Arjun stepped further inside, his eyes adjusted to the dim light, scanning the narrow aisles for any sign of life. At first, it seemed empty—only the hum of silence and the occasional rustle of pages disturbed the stillness.

Then, from behind a desk at the far end of the store, a woman emerged. She was draped in a dark shawl, her features partially obscured by the shadows cast from the low-hanging lamps. She watched him with a quiet intensity, her fingers lingering on the edge of a book she had been flipping through.

Women: "*You're late.*"

Arjun blinked, caught off guard. *Late?* He hadn't even known he was expected.

Arjun: "*I didn't know I had an appointment.*"

She tilted her head slightly, her gaze sharp yet unreadable.

Women: "*No one comes here by accident. You're looking for her, aren't you?*"

Arjun hesitated. "You know Natasha?"

The woman sighed, wiping her hands on her apron. "She used to come here a lot. She'd sit by the window and sketch. That was before... before everything happened."

Before what?

Arjun's pulse quickened. "What do you mean?"

She studied him for a moment, as if deciding whether he was someone who deserved to know. Finally, she gestured toward the back of the shop. "There's someone you should talk to."

In the small back room of the bookstore, dust motes swirled in the golden afternoon light. An older man sat in a leather armchair, flipping through a worn-out book. His gaze lifted when Arjun entered, and something passed through his eyes—a flicker of recognition, of sadness.

"You must be Arjun," the man said, closing his book. "Natasha spoke about you."

Arjun stiffened. "Who are you?"

The man exhaled, setting the book down on a weathered wooden table. "I was her professor. Years ago. Before the accident."

Arjun's breath caught in his throat. "Accident?"

The professor nodded slowly; his face shadowed with regret. "Natasha was in love once. With someone she thought she'd spend her life with. But love can be cruel, can't it?"

Arjun's chest tightened. He wanted to stop listening, to run out and find her, but the professor's voice held him captive.

"They were engaged," he continued. "And one night, they were driving back from a gallery opening. A drunk driver ran a red light."

Silence settled between them, thick and heavy, like grief had entered the room and refused to leave.

"She survived," the professor said softly. "He didn't."

Arjun swallowed hard, his hands trembling. The words felt like ice sinking into his skin.

"She never told me," he murmured, more to himself than to the professor.

"She doesn't talk about it," the professor said. "She carries it, though. Every day. In her sketches, in her silences. She's never stopped running from it."

Arjun clenched his jaw, the realization slicing through him like a blade. The way she hesitated whenever he got too close. The shadows in her gaze when she thought no one was looking. She wasn't just afraid of love—she was afraid of losing it. Again.

Natasha sat alone in a small motel room, staring at the rain beating against the window. It blurred the world outside, making everything look distant, unreal. That was how she felt—like she was slipping through time, trapped between the past and the future, unable to fully exist in either.

She shouldn't have left Arjun like that. He had been different, kind, and patient. He made her want to believe in something again. But every time she got close to someone, the past pulled her back like an unseen force, reminding her of the price love demanded.

She traced the scar on her wrist absentmindedly—a reminder of that night, of the moment everything had changed. The cold metal of the engagement ring had been pressed into her palm when they pulled her from the wreckage. She had held it so tightly that her skin had torn, the pain anchoring her in a reality too cruel to accept.

Her heart had been buried that night, somewhere between the shards of broken glass and the smell of burning metal. And she had never let herself dig it out.

A knock on the door startled her.

She didn't need to open it to know who it was.

"Natasha."

Arjun's voice was quiet, but it carried through the door like a plea.

She hesitated, her fingers hovering over the handle. Every part of her wanted to let him in, and every part of her was terrified of what that meant.

"Please," he said. "Just talk to me."

She squeezed her eyes shut, her breath shallow. The ghosts of her past whispered warnings in her ear, telling her to run, to disappear before it was too late. Before she let him become another name etched in the wreckage of her life.

But for the first time in years, she wasn't sure she wanted to listen.

The knock at the door lingered in the quiet of the motel room, pressing against Natasha's resolve like the weight of her past. She had spent so long running—from the pain, from the memories, from the fear of loving again. But Arjun's voice, steady and patient on the other side of the door, made her want to stop.

She didn't know how long she stood there, fingers curled around the handle, her heart hammering against her ribs. Part of her wanted to push the door open, to let him see her—truly see her, broken edges and all. The other part whispered the same warning she had carried for years: love only ends in loss.

But then she heard him sigh. Not with frustration, but something softer, something that sounded like understanding. "I'll wait, Natasha," he said, his voice gentle but certain. "For as long as it takes."

Something cracked inside her. She wasn't used to that—to someone waiting, to someone choosing to stay despite the shadows she carried. She wasn't sure she deserved it. But when she finally turned the handle and pulled the door open, Arjun was still there, hands in his pockets, eyes searching hers for permission.

And for the first time in years, she didn't run.

The days that followed were a slow unraveling. Natasha was used to hiding—behind her art, behind silence, behind the carefully constructed walls she had built over the years. But Arjun had a way of dismantling them without force, without expectations. He asked nothing of her except to be herself, and somehow, that was the most terrifying and beautiful thing she had ever encountered.

They left the motel together, but she didn't go back to her studio. Not yet. Instead, she let Arjun take her to the places she used to love—the quiet bookstore where she once lost herself in stories, the small café where she had filled her sketchbooks with strangers' faces. She hadn't stepped into these places since the accident, since her life had split into *before* and *after*.

At first, it was overwhelming. The past lurked in every corner, every familiar scent, every whispered memory. But Arjun never rushed her. He would sit across from her in the café, sipping his coffee, waiting until she was ready to speak. Some days, she said nothing at all. Others, the words tumbled out in uneven bursts—stories of love and loss, of the boy who had promised her forever and the night fate had stolen him away.

And Arjun listened. Always, he listened.

One evening, as they walked along the river, she finally asked the question that had been lingering between them. "Why do you stay?"

Arjun glanced at her, his expression unreadable. Then, after a long pause, he said, "Because you make me want to."

Natasha swallowed hard. "Even knowing everything? Knowing that I might never be whole again?"

He stopped walking, turning to face her fully. "Who says you have to be whole for someone to love you?"

She had no answer to that. Because for the first time, she wondered if maybe—just maybe—love wasn't about being unbroken. Maybe it was about being seen, even in the fragments.

When she finally stepped back into her studio, it felt different. It was the same space—the same unfinished paintings, the same scattered pencils—but something in her had shifted. The fear that had kept her away, that had convinced her she couldn't create without drowning in grief, was quieter now.

Arjun didn't follow her inside right away. He waited by the doorway, letting her take those first steps alone. And when she turned to him, something in her eyes must have changed, because he smiled—soft and knowing.

That night, she pulled out the sketchbook she had abandoned after meeting him. The pages were filled with him—his laughter, his quiet contemplation, the way his hands moved when he spoke. But on the last page, there was something new.

A sketch of herself.

Not the version of her that had been trapped in grief, but the version that was learning—slowly, hesitantly—to stay.

She showed it to Arjun without words. And he understood.

The change didn't happen all at once. Healing was not a straight path; it was a winding road with moments of doubt, moments where she still felt the urge to run. But every time she hesitated, Arjun was there—not to hold her back, but to remind her that she didn't have to do it alone.

She stopped counting the days. She stopped marking time by what she had lost and instead started measuring it by what she was building.

And one evening, as they stood on the rooftop of her studio, watching the city lights flicker below, she whispered the words that had once felt impossible.

"I want to stay."

Arjun turned to her, his expression unreadable for a moment. Then, slowly, a smile spread across his face—not triumphant, not expectant. Just full of quiet understanding.

"You already have," he said.

And for the first time, Natasha believed it.

Chapter 8:
Love in Small Moments

The days stretched into weeks, and what had begun as fleeting moments between Arjun and Natasha turned into something neither of them could ignore.

She became his muse, and he became her safe place.

Mornings were spent in Natasha's sunlit studio, where she painted in oversized shirts, barefoot and lost in her colors, while Arjun sat in the corner, typing away, the rhythm of his words matching the strokes of her brush. It was a quiet symphony of creation, two artists breathing life into their work in each other's presence. He often glanced at her, watching the way she would chew on her lower lip when deciding between shades of blue, or the way her eyes softened when she found just the right stroke. He wanted to write about her, to capture the way she painted her emotions onto the canvas, how her art spoke louder than her words ever did.

Afternoons were stolen in cafés and bookstores, where they argued over stories and philosophies, where she teased him for being too serious while he challenged her to embrace the chaos she painted so fearlessly. There was an ease between them, a push and pull that neither wanted to break. They moved through bookstores like they had known each other forever, flipping through pages, debating over authors, and getting lost in stories that mirrored their own uncertainties.

And the nights—those belonged to quiet rooftops, whispered confessions, and the kind of silences that said more than words ever could. They would sit with coffee cups growing cold beside them, the hum of the city below fading into a distant lullaby. Arjun would talk about his childhood, about the stories he wanted to write, the fears he never shared with anyone else. Natasha would listen, tracing patterns on the concrete, sometimes reaching for his hand when his words turned heavy. He wanted to tell her she was becoming his favorite story, but he feared if he spoke it aloud, she would disappear like a fleeting dream.

But love, even in its gentlest form, had a way of demanding the truth.

One evening, as they lay on the terrace of Natasha's studio, staring at the sky, Arjun turned to her and asked the question that had been weighing on his mind.

"What happens next?"

Natasha's fingers traced invisible patterns on the concrete. "In what?"

"In us."

She let out a breath, turning to face him. The city lights reflected in her dark eyes, and for the first time, she looked... uncertain.

"Arjun, you and I... we're different."

He frowned. "What does that mean?"

She sat up, pulling her knees to her chest. "It means... I don't know if I can be what you need."

His heart clenched. "And what do you think I need?"

"Someone who stays."

The words were quiet, but they cut through him like a blade.

"You think you're going to leave?" he asked, his voice steadier than he felt.

Natasha hesitated, her hands gripping the fabric of her shirt. "I don't know. But I don't want to promise you something I'm not sure I can give."

Arjun sat up, watching her. "Natasha, love isn't about certainty. It's about choosing someone, even when you don't have all the answers."

She looked at him then, her walls cracking just a little. "What if I choose you today, but I can't tomorrow?"

"Then I'll choose you again."

Her breath hitched. "You make it sound so simple."

"Because it is," he said softly. "Loving someone isn't about knowing how the story ends. It's about writing it together, one page at a time."

Natasha stared at him, her heart waging a silent war against her fears.

She had spent her whole life running—from expectations, from pain, from the idea of permanence. But Arjun… he wasn't asking her to be something she wasn't. He wasn't asking for forever.

He was just asking for now.

And maybe, for the first time, now was enough.

Without another word, she leaned in, pressing her lips against his.

It wasn't rushed, wasn't desperate. It was soft, uncertain, like a first brushstroke on a blank canvas.

And for the first time in a long time, Natasha didn't feel unfinished.

She felt like she was finally beginning.

But the past had a way of creeping in, even in moments of newfound clarity.

That night, long after Arjun had fallen asleep beside her on the terrace, Natasha lay awake, staring at the stars. Memories drifted in, unbidden and relentless—her mother's weary sighs, her father's disappearing footsteps, and the countless times she had packed and repacked her life in a suitcase, leaving behind the people who had dared to love her.

She remembered the summer she turned fifteen, when her father had called from a different country with a new life and a new family. He had promised to visit, but the months passed, and she learned the hard way that promises were just words. Her mother had never cried in front of her, but Natasha had seen the grief settle in her bones, the way she built walls so high that even love couldn't climb them. And Natasha had inherited those walls.

She traced circles on the fabric of Arjun's shirt, listening to the steady rhythm of his breathing. He was steady, certain, everything she had never known love to be. But what if she wasn't capable of that kind of love? What if, despite wanting to stay, she was doomed to leave?

Arjun stirred slightly, turning toward her, his arm draping over her waist as though, even in sleep, he knew she was slipping into her thoughts. She wanted to believe in the simplicity of his words—that love was about choosing someone again and again. But she had never known a love that wasn't fleeting. How could she trust it now?

Chapter 9:
The Art of Goodbyes

Arjun woke up to the scent of paint lingering in the air, the aroma of oil and turpentine interwoven with something softer, something distinctly Natasha. It clung to the sheets, the pillows, the very air he breathed. The golden hues of the early morning sun stretched across the studio, dappling the floorboards, illuminating the half-finished canvases Natasha had abandoned the night before.

But something felt different.

A stillness.

A wrongness.

His fingers reached instinctively to the other side of the bed, expecting warmth, the rise and fall of a familiar breath. Instead, the space was empty, cold.

A quiet unease settled in his chest. He sat up slowly, rubbing the sleep from his eyes, the remnants of dreams dissolving into an unfamiliar loneliness.

"Natasha?" His voice cracked in the silence.

Nothing.

His heart pounded as he threw off the sheets and placed his bare feet on the wooden floor, the chill seeping into his skin. He scanned the room, searching for the mess of dark hair, the half-smile she often greeted him with, and the eyes that held galaxies. The studio still bore traces of her—her brushes lay scattered, her coffee mug from last night still perched precariously on the table, and her perfume still ghosted through the air—but she was gone.

And then, he saw it.

A folded piece of paper sat beside his typewriter. His name was written on it in delicate, familiar handwriting.

His stomach clenched.

With trembling fingers, he reached for it, unfolding it with the same care one might handle a fragile thing on the verge of breaking.

Arjun,

I don't know how to write this, so I'll just say it—I'm leaving.

Not because I don't love you. But because I do.

I know you, Writer. You believe in forever. You believe love is a story that never ends. And I wish I could believe that, too. But I don't know how to stay. I never have.

I've spent my whole life running—running from expectations, from pain, from the fear of being left behind. And for the first time, you made me want to stop. You made me want to stay.

But wanting and knowing how to stay are two different things.

You once told me love isn't about knowing how the story ends, but Arjun... I can't be another unfinished page in your book. You deserve someone who stays without hesitation, without fear. And I'm afraid that's not me.

So, I'm doing the only thing I know how to do. I'm leaving before you can love me enough to make me stay.

Please don't hate me. Please don't wait for me.

But if you ever write about us—if you ever turn this into a story—don't make it a tragedy.

Because what we had? Even if it was fleeting, even if it was unfinished… it was real.

And that's enough.

—Natasha

The letter slipped from Arjun's fingers, floating to the floor as if the weight of its words had become too much for even the paper to hold.

For a long moment, he just stood there, staring at it, as if by some miracle, the ink would rearrange itself, the meaning would change, the reality would shift.

But the city outside continued its symphony of indifference—cars honked, birds chattered, and the world spun on, uncaring of the fact that his had just shattered.

A breath. Then another. But each felt heavier than the last.

He stumbled backward until he found the edge of the bed and sank onto it, his fingers threading through his hair, gripping, pulling. His chest ached—not the sharp, immediate pain of a wound, but the slow, suffocating kind. The kind that settled in the bones and refused to leave.

She was gone.

The woman who had painted his world in color had left him with nothing but shades of gray.

Hours passed, or maybe just minutes—time blurred, losing all meaning. He found himself tracing the letters of her note over and over, as if memorizing the strokes of her hand might bring her back. As if understanding the pain behind her words might make it hurt less.

But it didn't.

Memories rushed in, unbidden and unstoppable. The way she used to hum while she painted, lost in her own world. The way her laughter filled up every empty space. The way she curled into him at night, seeking warmth, seeking safety.

The way she had loved him, fiercely, yet always with the quiet undertone of something fleeting.

He should have known.

Maybe, in some part of him, he had always known.

She had been a fire—brilliant, consuming, impossible to hold for long. And yet, he had let himself believe, just for a moment, that he could be the one to keep her burning.

He rose on unsteady feet, the weight of exhaustion pressing on him. He walked to his desk, his typewriter waiting, silent and patient, the way she hadn't been.

The letter lay beside it, its presence a whisper of what once was. With a deep breath, he picked it up and placed it carefully to the side. Then, with trembling hands, he rolled a fresh sheet of paper into the machine.

His fingers hovered over the keys.

A breath. A pause.

Then, he began to type.

"She loved like an unfinished painting—messy, beautiful, and impossible to forget."

Because Natasha had asked for one thing.

She had asked him not to make this a tragedy.

So, he wouldn't.

Even if it broke him.

Chapter 10:
The Story that Stayed

Days passed. Then weeks.

Natasha was gone, but she was everywhere.

Arjun saw her in the way the sunlight hit his coffee cup in the morning. In the unfinished paintings she had left behind, their colors frozen mid-motion. In the city streets they had wandered together, her laughter echoed in his memory.

But mostly, he saw her in his words.

His novel, the one that had been stuck in limbo for so long, began to take shape. The story poured out of him like ink from a broken pen, raw, and relentless. He wrote about love that felt like a sunset—beautiful, fleeting, and impossible to hold on to. He wrote about a girl who painted the world in color but was afraid of staying in one place long enough to dry.

And he wrote about a boy who loved her anyway.

Some nights, he hated her for leaving, for making him believe in something only to take it away. Other nights, he understood.

But no matter what, he couldn't stop loving her.

One evening, weeks after she had disappeared, Arjun found himself back at the beach where they had once sat together, her fingers tracing patterns in the sand.

The sky was painted in soft pinks and purples, the waves crashing gently against the shore. He reached into his pocket and pulled out the seashell she had once held in her hands.

"Then don't stay," he had told her that night. "But take something with you."

He wondered if she had.

Did she carry pieces of him the way he carried pieces of her? Did she ever wake up and reach for him, only to remember he wasn't there?

Or had she already moved on, leaving him behind like another unfinished painting?

He closed his eyes, gripping the shell tightly.

And then, as if the universe had heard his silent plea, a voice cut through the evening air.

"Arjun."

His heart stopped.

Slowly, he turned.

And there she was.

Natasha.

Standing just a few feet away, barefoot in the sand, looking at him like she had never left at all.

Silence fell between them, thick with the weight of everything unsaid. The wind tugged at her hair, strands whipping across her face, but she didn't move to push them away. She only watched him, as if she were memorizing every detail, as if she were afraid he might vanish if she blinked.

Arjun swallowed hard. "You came back."

She exhaled a shaky breath. "I never really left."

He let out a hollow laugh, shaking his head. "That's funny, because it sure felt like you did."

Natasha stepped closer. "I know. And I'm sorry."

Her voice was barely a whisper, but it cut through him like a blade. He had imagined this moment a thousand times—what he would say, what she would say. In some versions, he was angry. In others, he begged her to stay. But standing here now, all he could feel was exhaustion. He had spent so long chasing the ghosts of her, carrying the weight of her absence like an anchor, and now she was here.

He wasn't sure if it was enough.

"Why?" The word was small, but it carried everything—his pain, his longing, and his hope. "Why did you leave?"

Natasha wrapped her arms around herself, her gaze flickering toward the ocean. "Because I was scared."

"Of what?"

"Of you. Of this." She gestured between them, her voice trembling. "Of what it meant to love you."

Arjun clenched his jaw, looking away. The waves crashed, filling the silence between them. He wanted to say so many things—to tell her how much she had hurt him, to ask her why she had let him love her if she was only going to run. But all that came out was, "Did you ever think about me?"

Her breath hitched. "Every day."

Something inside him cracked. "Then why didn't you come back sooner?"

"I didn't know if you wanted me to."

His chest ached. "You didn't know? Natasha, I—" He ran a hand through his hair, exhaling sharply. "I would have crossed oceans for you."

"I know." Her eyes shone with unshed tears. "And that terrified me."

Silence stretched between them again, heavy and unyielding. Then, hesitantly, she reached out, her fingers brushing against his. It was the lightest of touches, but it sent a fire through his veins.

"Do you still love me?" She asked, her voice barely audible over the waves.

Arjun's throat tightened. He wanted to lie. To tell her no, that he had moved on, that he had forgotten her the way she had left him behind. But he had never been good at lying.

"Yes."

Natasha closed her eyes, exhaling as if she had been holding her breath for weeks. When she opened them again, they were filled with something raw, something fragile. "I love you too."

He let out a breathless laugh, shaking his head. "That doesn't change anything."

"I know."

But still, she didn't move away.

Neither did he.

The night deepened around them, the stars blinking awake in the sky. They sat side by side in the sand, shoulders touching, neither speaking.

The weight of their love hung between them, both a comfort and a burden.

Finally, Natasha broke the silence. "Tell me about your book."

Arjun hesitated, then sighed. "It's about a boy who loved a girl who was afraid to stay."

She flinched. "Arjun…"

He shook his head. "It's okay. It's the truth."

She was quiet for a long time before she whispered, "Does she come back?"

He turned to look at her, his gaze searching hers. "I don't know yet."

A tear slipped down her cheek. "Maybe she wants to."

He reached out, catching the tear with his thumb. His voice was soft, aching. "Then maybe she should."

And in that moment, as the ocean whispered its secrets and the night wrapped around them like a promise, they both knew—this story wasn't over yet.

Not even close.

Chapter 11:
Choosing Love

Arjun didn't let go of Natasha for a long time.

He held her as if he were anchoring her to this moment, to him.

He wasn't sure if it was the sound of the waves crashing around them or the way her heartbeat matched his, but for the first time in weeks, he felt whole.

When he finally pulled back, he searched her eyes, as if trying to memorize every piece of her before she could slip away again.

"Tell me the truth, Natasha," he said quietly. "Are you staying?"

She nodded, but he needed more than that.

"Not just for now. Not just until it gets hard," he pressed. "Are you staying for good?"

Natasha took a shaky breath. "Yes."

He studied her, waiting for hesitation, for doubt. But there was none.

Still, he had to ask, "What changed?"

She exhaled, looking away for a moment, gathering her thoughts. "I kept telling myself that leaving was the right thing to do. That you deserved someone better. Someone who wasn't afraid of love. But every day without you felt like losing a part of myself."

She glanced at him, her voice softer now. "And then, I realized... I don't want to live in a world where you're just a memory."

Arjun's throat tightened.

"I don't know how to do this perfectly," she admitted, stepping closer. "But I want to try. With you."

His fingers brushed against hers, tentative, testing. "No running?"

She intertwined her fingers with his, gripping tightly. "No running."

Arjun let out a shaky laugh, his heart pounding.

And then, as if the universe had been holding its breath, he kissed her.

It wasn't a kiss of desperation or uncertainty. It wasn't about erasing the past or making promises about the future.

It was a kiss of choice.

Natasha was choosing him. And, for Arjun, that was enough.

The Days That Followed

The days that followed weren't perfect.

Natasha still had moments when she hesitated, when she caught herself falling too fast. Arjun still had moments when he feared she'd wake up one day and change her mind.

But love wasn't about never being afraid. It was about choosing someone despite the fear.

And they chose each other.

One evening, as they sat on the rooftop of Natasha's studio, Arjun glanced at the painting she was working on.

It was a portrait.

Of him.

But this time, it wasn't unfinished.

Natasha caught him staring and smiled. "I finally completed one."

He looked at her, something warm settling in his chest. "Yeah," he murmured. "You did."

Not just the painting. Not just the love story.

But she had finally mastered the art of staying.

And in that moment, Arjun knew—some love stories weren't meant to be perfect.

They were meant to be real.

And theirs was.

Chapter 12:
A Love that was Never Meant to Stay

Arjun kissed Natasha like he was trying to memorize her—every sigh, every touch, every fragile moment between them.

And for a second, he allowed himself to believe.

To believe that love could be enough. That choosing each other meant they would last.

But love had never been kind to him. And Natasha... Natasha had never known how to stay.

The morning was soft, the kind that carried the illusion of peace.

Arjun woke up to the faint scent of paint and salt air. He turned over, expecting to find Natasha beside him, tangled in the sheets.

But she wasn't there.

The bed was cold.

A quiet dread curled inside him as he sat up, scanning the room. The studio was untouched, as if she had never been there at all.

And then, he saw it.

A single piece of paper, placed beside his typewriter.

His heart pounded as he reached for it.

Arjun,

I know I promised. I know I said I wouldn't run.

But some people aren't meant to be caged by love, no matter how much they wish they could be.

I wanted to stay. I wanted to be the person who could wake up every morning beside you without wondering if she belonged somewhere else.

But I'm not her.

You told me once that love isn't about knowing the ending, but writing it together. But, Arjun... this was always going to be our ending.

I was never meant to stay.

I hope one day, you'll forgive me.

I hope one day, you'll write a story where we don't end like this.

But this? This is the only way I know how to love you.

By leaving before I break you even more.

- Natasha

Arjun stared at the letter, his vision blurring.

He waited for the anger to come. The betrayal. The hate.

But all he felt was the same aching emptiness he had felt the first time she left.

The worst part?

He had believed her.

He had *let* himself believe her.

And now, she was gone.

For real, this time.

The woman who had taught him how to paint with feeling had left him with nothing but an unfinished love story.

Arjun clenched his fists, his chest tightening with the kind of grief that had no name.

Then, slowly, he reached for his typewriter, rolling in a fresh sheet of paper.

His fingers trembled as he began to type.

"She loved like a storm—beautiful, fleeting, and destined to leave destruction in her wake."

And just like that, he wrote the final chapter of their story.

Chapter 13:
Some People are Meant to be Ghosts

Arjun read the letter once. Then twice.

His fingers trembled as he traced the edges of the paper, as if holding it tighter he could somehow have her back.

But she was gone.

Again.

For real this time.

The room was silent except for the slow, hollow pounding of his heart. Outside, the city moved on—cars honking, people laughing, life continuing as if nothing had happened.

But Arjun's world had ended.

He stood up abruptly, the chair scraping against the wooden floor. His breath was shallow, uneven. He turned toward the paintings Natasha had left behind, the colors so full of life.

Lies.

All of it. Lies.

She had painted him into her world, made him believe he belonged there. And then, just like that, she had erased him.

His eyes landed on the unfinished portrait of him—the one she had promised was complete.

A sharp laugh bubbled in his throat.

Of course. Of course, even her art was a lie.

Something inside him snapped.

Before he could stop himself, his fist shot out, colliding with the canvas. The impact sent it crashing to the ground, the wooden frame splintering. His breath was ragged, his chest heaving. But the pain in his knuckles was nothing compared to the one spreading through his ribs.

He turned to the desk, his eyes burning. His typewriter sat there, waiting, as if it expected him to turn this heartbreak into poetry.

But there was nothing beautiful about being abandoned.

Not again.

Not by *her*.

The night was cruel.

The alcohol burned as it slid down his throat, but he welcomed it. He needed something to drown out the memories, to silence the echoes of her laughter in his mind.

He stumbled through the streets, lost in a haze of neon lights and shadows. He barely noticed the rain beginning to fall, soaking through his clothes.

His feet carried him somewhere familiar—an old bridge overlooking the city.

The last place he had ever seen his mother.

The night she had collapsed right in front of him, her body frail, her breath coming in sharp gasps. He had been too young to understand, too small to do anything but scream her name. By the time help arrived, it was too late.

And then his father left too—not in the same tragic way, but in a way that left just as many scars. He had called it duty, responsibility. A job that couldn't allow for attachments. But to Arjun, the night Natasha had walked away and never came back, it had felt like confirmation.

Arjun leaned against the railing, gripping the cold metal as a bitter realization settled in his chest.

People didn't leave him by accident.

They left because they wanted to.

Because they looked at him—his love, his devotion, his unshakable belief in forever—and they *chose* to walk away.

His father.

His mother.

And now, Natasha.

A sob broke from his lips, raw and unfiltered. The wind howled around him, and for the first time in years, he let himself *feel* the weight of it all.

The weight of never being enough to make someone stay.

He closed his eyes, the city below blurring into a sea of lights.

Would it hurt?

Would it feel like flying, even for a second?

Or would it be just another unfinished ending?

He loosened his grip on the railing.

And then—

A hand.

Soft. Familiar.

Grabbing his wrist.

His eyes snapped open.

And there she was.

Natasha.

Soaked from the rain, her chest rising and falling as if she had been running. Her fingers were ice-cold against his skin, but her grip was *firm*.

"Don't," she whispered, her voice breaking.

His throat tightened. "Why do you care?"

Her face crumpled. "Because I never stopped."

Arjun let out a broken laugh. "Then why did you leave?"

Tears mixed with raindrops on her cheeks. "Because I thought you'd be better without me."

He searched her face, looking for the lie.

And for the first time, there wasn't one.

She was just as lost as he was.

He clenched his jaw, his body shaking. "You don't get to decide what's best for me."

Natasha's grip tightened. "Then let me fix it."

Arjun's breath caught. "How?"

She swallowed, stepping closer. "By staying."

His chest ached. He wanted to believe her. God, he *needed* to believe her.

But he was so, so *tired* of believing in things that weren't real.

So, he looked at her one last time.

And then, with rain soaking through his clothes, with her fingers still gripping his wrist—

He let go.

Chapter 14:
Love, Loss, and the Weight of Goodbye

The world slowed.

Raindrops fell in heavy sheets, and the city blurred into nothing but a mess of lights and shadows. The moment Arjun let go, Natasha's breath hitched in her throat.

And then—

She lunged.

Her hands, slick with rain, barely managed to grip his arm. The weight of him nearly pulled them both over the edge, but she *held on*.

"Arjun!" she screamed, her voice cracking.

His fingers trembled, slipping through hers, as the wind roaring in his ears. He looked up at her—at the woman who had broken him, who had left him, and yet... who had still come back.

Why?

"Let me go," he whispered, his voice barely audible over the storm.

Natasha's eyes burned with fury. "No."

Her grip tightened as she planted her feet against the slick pavement, pulling with every ounce of strength she had left. He could see it—the raw desperation in her eyes, the silent plea for him to *hold on*.

But Arjun had spent his whole life holding on to people who didn't stay.

He didn't know how to do it anymore.

His body jerked downward, and for a terrifying second, he thought she would let go.

But she didn't.

With one final, breathless effort, she pulled him back over the railing, sending them both crashing onto the cold pavement.

The world tilted.

Arjun lay on his back, the rain hammering against his skin, his lungs burning from the weight of everything. Natasha collapsed beside him, gasping for breath, her soaked hair sticking to her face.

For a long time, neither of them spoke.

Then, through gritted teeth, she punched his chest.

Hard.

"You idiot," she choked out, her hands trembling.

He winced. "Natasha—"

"No," she snapped, sitting up. "You don't get to do this. You don't get to decide that you're not worth saving. Not when I—"

Her voice broke.

Arjun turned his head, watching her through the blur of rain. "Not when you what?"

She swallowed hard, closing her eyes.

And then, in the quietest voice, she said, "Not when I love you."

His breath caught.

But before he could say anything, before he could even *process* those words, a pair of headlights pierced through the rain.

A car.

Coming fast.

Too fast.

The realization hit him too late.

"Natasha—"

The sound of screeching tires ripped through the night.

Then, everything shattered.

Chapter 15:
The Story that Ended too Soon

White walls. A steady beeping sound. The sterile scent of antiseptic.

Arjun's world came back to him in pieces.

Pain.

A dull, numbing pain spread through his ribs, his head pounding with every heartbeat. He tried to move, but his body felt heavy, his limbs foreign.

He blinked against the harsh hospital lights.

That's when he saw her.

Natasha.

Lying in the hospital bed beside his, unnaturally still.

His breath caught as he took in the bandages wrapped around her forehead, the IV dripping into her arm. Bruises trailed down her skin like shadows, but her chest rose and fell in a steady rhythm.

Alive.

She was alive.

A sharp breath rattled through him as he turned his head toward the door, where a nurse was speaking in hushed tones to a doctor.

"... She lost a lot of blood," the nurse murmured. "We're lucky she made it through surgery."

"She hasn't woken up yet?" the doctor asked.

The nurse shook her head. "No. But it's only been a few hours. The next 24 hours are critical."

Arjun's hands clenched into fists.

This was his fault.

If he hadn't been so lost, so broken, she never would have been there. She never would have been on that road, in that moment.

And now, because of him, she was *fighting for her life*.

He swallowed the lump in his throat, his eyes burning.

"I love you."

Her voice echoed in his mind, over and over, as if the universe was forcing him to remember.

And now, she might never wake up to hear him say it back.

A ragged sob tore from his chest.

He reached for her hand, threading his fingers through hers, ignoring the pain that shot through his body.

"Please wake up," he whispered. "Please."

But Natasha didn't move.

She just lay there, frozen in time.

And for the first time in his life, Arjun realized—

Loving someone wasn't about the moments you *had*.

It was about the moments you *lost*.

And sometimes, love wasn't a promise.

It was a tragedy.

Chapter 16:
Letting Go of what Hurts

The beeping of the heart monitor was steady. Unchanging.

For days, Arjun sat beside Natasha's bed, watching her breathe, waiting for the moment her eyes would open.

And when they finally did, it was like the entire world held its breath.

At first, she blinked slowly, her gaze unfocused, as if she were trying to piece together where she was. Then, her eyes met his.

And everything cracked inside him.

"Arjun?" Her voice was hoarse, barely above a whisper.

His throat tightened, but he forced himself to nod. "Yeah," he murmured. "I'm here."

Her fingers twitched against the sheets, as if she wanted to reach for him, but she was too weak. "What... what happened?"

He swallowed. "You saved me."

Natasha's brows furrowed, confusion flickering in her eyes. "The accident... I remember the lights, the sound. I thought—"

She cut herself off, her expression shifting from confusion to realization.

"You thought you were going to die," Arjun finished for her.

Natasha didn't answer. She just looked at him, eyes searching his face, as if she already knew what was coming.

Because Arjun wasn't the same person she had pulled back from that bridge.

Something in him had *changed*.

And he knew what he had to do.

Even if it tore him apart.

He exhaled shakily, leaning forward, gripping her hand gently. "Natasha…"

Her fingers curled slightly around his, as if she already knew he was about to say something that would shatter them both.

"You should hate me," he whispered. "You almost died because of me."

She shook her head instantly. "No—"

"I can't do this anymore," he cut in, his voice breaking. "I can't keep waiting for the next time you'll leave. The next time I won't be enough. And I *sure as hell* can't keep being the reason you get hurt."

Tears welled in her eyes. "You think this is your fault?"

Arjun let out a broken laugh, rubbing a hand over his face. "Isn't it?"

Natasha tried to sit up, but pain flashed across her face, and she winced. "Arjun, no," she breathed. "It was an accident—"

"But we are not an accident." His voice was raw, edged with something dangerously close to regret. "We are a mistake that keeps repeating itself."

Her breath hitched. "You don't mean that."

Arjun looked at her for a long moment.

Then, quietly, he said, "Yes, I do."

Tears slipped down Natasha's cheeks, but she didn't wipe them away. "I love you," she whispered. "I *chose* you."

He let out a shaky breath, his heart screaming at him to stay, to fight for her, to make this work.

But loving someone didn't mean breaking them in the process.

And if he stayed, they would *keep* breaking each other.

He reached forward, gently brushing a strand of hair from her face, his fingers lingering just long enough to memorize her warmth.

"I love you too," he admitted, his voice barely above a whisper.

Then, he stood.

Natasha's face crumpled. "Please—"

But Arjun shook his head. "Goodbye, Natasha."

And before she could beg him to stay, before his heart could betray him—

He walked out the door.

Out of the hospital.

Out of her life.

And this time, *he* was the one who left.

Months later, Arjun sat alone in his apartment, staring at the last page of his manuscript.

The story of a love that was never meant to last.

A love that burned too bright, too fast, and left nothing but ashes.

He hovered over the final sentence, his fingers trembling.

Then, he typed the words he never wanted to write.

"Some love stories aren't meant to have a happy ending. Some are just meant to be felt—once, deeply, and never again."

He closed the laptop, exhaling slowly.

And just like that, their story was over.

Chapter 17:
Love in the Silence

The bookstore smelled the same.

Old paper, fresh ink, the faint aroma of coffee drifting in from the corner café.

Natasha stepped inside, her heart hammering in her chest. It had been months since she had last seen him. Months since he had walked away, leaving nothing behind but the weight of his words—words that now sat in her hands, bound between the pages of his book.

She had read it cover to cover, her fingers tracing every sentence, as if she could feel him in the ink.

"Some love stories aren't meant to have a happy ending. Some are just meant to be felt—once, deeply, and never again."

But Arjun had been wrong.

Because even after all this time, she still *felt* him.

She still loved him.

And maybe that was enough.

She walked past the shelves, her breath catching when she saw him.

Arjun.

Standing exactly where he had been the first time they met, fingers skimming over the books, lost in thought.

But this time, he was holding a copy of his own story.

Natasha took a slow, measured breath, her fingers tightening around her copy. She stepped forward, the sound of her boots against the wooden floor the only thing breaking the silence.

He looked up.

Their eyes met.

The air shifted.

For a long moment, neither of them spoke.

No grand gestures. No dramatic speeches.

Just the quiet hum of something unfinished.

Natasha exhaled softly and held up the book. "I read it."

Arjun's grip tightened around his copy. "Yeah?" His voice was careful, unreadable.

She nodded. "You got it wrong."

His brows furrowed, his gaze searching hers. "What do you mean?"

Natasha took another step closer, closing the space between them.

"You wrote that love isn't always meant to last," she murmured. "But even after all this time, I still love you."

His breath hitched, his fingers trembling.

She reached out slowly, giving him the chance to pull away.

But he didn't.

Her fingers brushed against his, tentative and uncertain. And then—

He *let her.*

Their hands met, fitting together like they always had, like time had never unraveled them in the first place.

Arjun swallowed, his voice barely above a whisper. "And if we break each other again?"

She smiled softly, her grip firm. "Then we start over."

He looked at her for a long moment, the weight of everything unsaid hanging between them.

And then—

He squeezed her hand.

No promises. No certainty of forever.

Just love, in the spaces in between.

And for them, that was enough.

A Question Left Unanswered

The rain had started again by the time they stepped out of the bookstore.

Soft. Gentle. Nothing like the storm that had nearly torn them apart.

Natasha tilted her face up, letting the droplets kiss her skin, a small smile playing at her lips. "It's always raining when we find our way back to each other."

Arjun glanced at her, his expression unreadable. "Maybe it's a sign."

She turned to him, her fingers still entwined with his. "A sign of what?"

He didn't answer right away. Instead, he studied her—the way her eyes searched his, the way her fingers traced small circles against his palm.

Then, he did something that made her breath catch.

He reached out and tucked a strand of damp hair behind her ear.

It was nothing grand. Nothing dramatic.

But it was *everything*.

Arjun exhaled, his voice barely above a whisper. "That this isn't over."

Natasha's heart pounded.

She didn't ask what he meant.

Because she knew.

They were a story that refused to end. A love that unraveled, rewrote itself, and stitched back together in ways they couldn't control.

But this time...

Would it be different?

Before she could say anything, a car horn blared from across the street.

Arjun stiffened.

Natasha followed his gaze—and that's when she saw it.

A man.

Standing beneath a streetlight, watching them.

Dressed in black. Unmoving.

And in his hand—

A copy of Arjun's book.

A chill crawled up Natasha's spine. "Do you know him?"

Arjun's jaw tightened. "No."

But something in his eyes said otherwise.

Before she could press further, the man turned and disappeared into the night.

Natasha looked back at Arjun.

For the first time since finding him again, something *unspoken* passed between them.

Something heavier than love.

Something that whispered—*this wasn't the end.*

It was just the beginning.

The Beginning of an Unfinished Story

The rain fell harder now, washing the city in streaks of silver.

Natasha shivered, suddenly cold despite Arjun's hand still wrapped around hers.

The man was gone. Disappearing into the night like a shadow. But the unease he left behind lingered, thick in the air.

She turned back to Arjun, searching his face. "You're sure you don't know him?"

He hesitated. Just for a second.

It was enough.

Natasha's stomach twisted. "Arjun."

His grip on her hand tightened, but he didn't meet her eyes. Instead, he exhaled slowly and turned away, running a hand through his rain-drenched hair. "It's nothing."

A lie.

She knew him too well to believe otherwise.

And yet, before she could press him, a gust of wind blew past them, sending a small piece of paper fluttering against her ankle.

Frowning, she bent down and picked it up.

A note.

Handwritten. The ink smudged from the rain, but still legible.

Her breath caught as she read the words.

"Some stories were never meant to be written."

The paper trembled between her fingers.

She looked up at Arjun, her heart hammering in her chest. "Tell me the truth."

His jaw clenched, his eyes dark and unreadable.

"Not here," he said. "Not now."

Lightning flashed in the distance, illuminating the city for just a moment—long enough for Natasha to catch the flicker of something she had never seen in Arjun before.

Fear.

And just like that, she realized—

This wasn't just about them.

This wasn't just about love.

This was about something *bigger*.

Something she wasn't ready for.

But it was too late.

Because they were already part of the story.

And whoever had left that note?

They were watching.

Waiting.

Chapter 18:
The Unfinished Chapter

The note lay on Natasha's nightstand, untouched since that night. She hadn't thrown it away. She couldn't.

Because deep down, she knew—this wasn't over.

She traced the smudged words with her fingertips, her mind replaying the moment Arjun had refused to answer her. The way his body had tensed, the flicker of fear in his eyes.

He was hiding something.

And whoever had left that note knew exactly what it was.

Natasha glanced at the copy of Arjun's book beside it, her chest tightening. The book that had led her back to him. The book that told their story—except now, she was starting to wonder if she had read it all wrong.

Because maybe Arjun's words weren't just about love and loss.

Maybe they were a warning.

Her phone buzzed, pulling her out of her thoughts.

A message.

From an unknown number.

"You should've let him go. Some stories don't have happy endings."

Natasha's breath caught in her throat.

Her hands trembled as she looked toward the window. The street below was quiet, empty except for the soft glow of streetlights.

But suddenly, she felt like she wasn't alone.

Like someone was still watching.

Waiting.

The rain started again, tapping against the glass like a whispered promise.

She closed her eyes, gripping the note in her hands.

She had thought this was the end of their story.

But now, she knew—

It was only the beginning.

Chapter 19:
Shadows Between Us

The rain hadn't stopped.

Natasha stood at the window, the city blurred behind streaks of water on the glass. Her reflection stared back at her—wide eyes, pale skin, shadows beneath her lashes. The note still sat on her nightstand, the words carved into her mind like scars.

"You should've let him go. Some stories don't have happy endings."

She tightened her arms around herself, her breath fogging the glass. Somewhere in the dark, someone was watching. Someone who knew too much. About Arjun. About their story. About things Natasha didn't even understand yet.

A soft knock at the door made her flinch. Her heart hammered painfully as she turned.

"Natasha?"

Arjun's voice.

She hesitated, but then the door creaked open, and he stepped inside. His dark hair was wet from the rain, droplets sliding down his sharp jawline. His eyes—stormy and guarded—locked onto hers.

"You've been standing there for an hour," he said quietly.

She swallowed hard. "I couldn't sleep."

Arjun's gaze dropped to the note on the nightstand. His jaw tensed. He crossed the room and picked it up, his fingers brushing against the ink-streaked paper. His face hardened.

"Who sent this?" Natasha asked.

He didn't answer.

"Arjun." Her voice was sharper now.

He slowly lowered the note, his thumb running over the edge. "It doesn't matter."

"It *does* matter," she snapped. "You know who left this, don't you?"

He hesitated. The muscle in his jaw twitched.

"Arjun."

He closed his eyes for a brief second, his shoulders rising and falling with a measured breath. Then he opened them—and the haunted look in his gaze made her heart turn to ice.

"I thought it was over," he said, voice rough. "I thought walking away would be enough."

"What are you talking about?"

His gaze sharpened. He stepped toward her, his hand sliding along her jaw. His thumb brushed her cheekbone, a quiet desperation in his touch.

"You shouldn't have followed me that day," he whispered.

Her breath hitched. "Why?"

"Because now you're part of it."

The tension in the room coiled tight around them, electric and dangerous.

"Part of *what*?" she whispered.

Arjun's hand slid down her face, his thumb lingering on her lip before falling away. His eyes darkened, shadowed with something deeper than fear.

"Years ago," he said softly, "Before I wrote the book, I was part of something."

"What kind of something?"

His mouth tightened. "Something dangerous."

Her blood chilled.

He took a step back, rubbing a hand through his rain-slick hair. "When I left, I thought they'd let me go. I thought if I disappeared—if I cut all ties—it would end there."

She shook her head, her pulse racing. "But it didn't."

Arjun's eyes met hers. His silence was answer enough.

"And now they know about me," Natasha said, her voice a strained whisper.

A knock at the window made them both freeze.

Natasha's head whipped toward the sound.

Outside, through the rain-slick glass—

A figure stood beneath the streetlight.

Dressed in black.

Holding a copy of Arjun's book.

Arjun cursed under his breath, crossing the room in two steps. He grabbed Natasha's arm and pulled her away from the window.

"We have to go," he said.

"Arjun—"

"No." His voice was sharper now, cold, and edged with panic. "Get your coat."

She resisted, fear cutting through the haze of confusion. "Who is that?"

"They don't leave warnings," he said darkly. "Not unless they're already close."

She hesitated, torn between fear and anger. "If you know who it is, tell me."

Arjun's hand closed around her wrist. His eyes were sharp, almost dangerous. "Trust me."

Her chest tightened. "How can I trust you when you're keeping secrets?"

The knock came again. Louder.

Three slow taps.

"Natasha." Arjun's voice softened. "Please."

Her breath hitched. And despite everything—despite the cold weight of fear in her chest—she nodded.

Arjun led her toward the door, his hand wrapped tightly around hers. He opened it and they slipped into the dark hallway. The rain hammered the windows as they moved through the quiet apartment building.

They reached the stairwell when Arjun suddenly stopped.

At the bottom of the stairs, a figure stood.

Not the man from the street.

This one was closer.

Wearing black gloves. A hood shadowing their face.

Arjun's grip tightened on Natasha's hand.

"Don't move," he said softly.

The figure tilted their head. Slowly. Deliberately.

Then—

They dropped something at their feet.

A photograph.

It fluttered through the air and landed between them.

Natasha's pulse spiked. She bent down slowly, her fingers trembling as she picked it up.

Her breath froze.

It was a picture of her and Arjun—taken earlier that night as they stood in the bookstore.

"Arjun..." Her voice cracked.

He reached for her hand—but suddenly, the figure turned and vanished into the stairwell.

Arjun cursed and took off after them.

"Arjun!" Natasha called, but he was already running.

She stumbled down the stairs after him, her heart pounding so hard it blurred her thoughts.

She reached the bottom just in time to see Arjun standing in the rain-drenched alley outside. Alone.

The figure was gone.

Arjun's chest heaved. He turned toward her, rain dripping from his hair. His eyes were sharp and dark.

"This isn't random," he said. "They know everything."

Natasha clutched the photo to her chest. "What do they want?"

Arjun's gaze darkened.

"They want the story."

Her stomach twisted. "The book?"

He shook his head.

"No." His voice was low, deadly.

"They want the truth."

Natasha's breath hitched. "What truth?"

Arjun stepped closer, his wet fingers brushing against her cheek. His eyes—burning and dangerous—locked onto hers.

"The story you read?" he whispered. "It wasn't fiction."

Her heart stilled.

He leaned in, his breath warm against her ear.

"It was a confession."

Chapter 20:
Whispers Beneath the Surface

The photograph sat between them on the small table. Its edges curled slightly from the rain, the image glistening under the dim glow of the table lamp. Natasha stared at it, her heart thundering in her chest.

It was impossible. A picture of them, taken that night at the bookstore.

Arjun sat across from her, his hands clasped together, his gaze hard and focused. The storm outside rattled the windows, filling the silence between them with low, steady percussion.

"You're telling me," Natasha's voice broke, "That the book—*your book*—was a confession?"

Arjun's eyes darkened. "Yes."

Her pulse spiked. "A confession to what?"

He hesitated, his jaw tightening. His eyes flicked toward the photograph, the shadows along his face sharpened by the lamplight.

"Arjun."

His gaze slid back to hers. "You need to stop asking questions."

She pushed the photograph toward him. "I can't. Not after this."

He exhaled, his hand brushing over the image as though he could erase it. "They're watching us now."

"*Who* is watching us?"

A flicker of frustration crossed his face. He stood suddenly, pacing toward the window. The rain streaked down the glass in shimmering trails. His silhouette cut sharply against the cold light outside.

"You don't understand," he said, his voice low.

"Then make me understand!"

His shoulders tensed. Slowly, he turned toward her, his face carved in shadow. His eyes—a storm of dark emotion—locked onto hers.

"I told you I was part of something."

Natasha stood, crossing the space between them. Her hands trembled as she reached for him, her fingertips brushing his wrist. He didn't pull away.

"What was it?" she whispered.

Arjun's eyes flashed with something darker than fear. Something colder.

"A society," he said quietly.

Natasha's blood chilled. "What kind of society?"

Arjun's lips curled in a dark, humorless smile. "The kind that doesn't forgive loose ends."

Her chest constricted painfully. "What did you do?"

His gaze sharpened. His hand rose, his thumb brushing the curve of her jaw. His touch was achingly gentle despite the hardness in his eyes.

"I told them a story," he said.

Her heart hammered. "The book."

Arjun nodded. "Every story has a hidden truth. Mine was... dangerous."

"Dangerous how?"

He leaned in, his forehead nearly touching hers. His breath ghosted over her lips, his fingers tightening on her jaw.

"Because it wasn't mine to tell."

The weight of his words settled into her chest like lead.

Natasha's lips parted. "Then why did you write it?"

Arjun's eyes closed briefly, his brow tightening as though the memory was too sharp, too close.

"Because they thought I was dead," he whispered. "And I wanted them to stay that way."

Her breath hitched. "But now they know you're alive."

His eyes opened—dark and sharp as cut glass. "And now they know about you."

A sharp knock at the door made them both freeze.

Natasha's breath caught in her throat. She turned toward the sound as Arjun's hand shot out, grabbing her wrist and pulling her behind him.

The knock came again. Three slow, deliberate taps.

Arjun's body tensed. His free hand slid toward the drawer in the side table, his fingers curling around something inside.

"Stay behind me," he murmured.

Natasha's heart thudded painfully as Arjun crossed the room. He unlocked the door—but didn't open it.

"Who is it?"

Silence.

The tension between them thickened, sharp as wire.

And then—

A piece of paper slid beneath the door.

Arjun's jaw clenched. He bent down slowly, picked it up, and unfolded it.

Natasha watched as his face darkened. The muscles in his jaw tightened, his fingers curling around the edges of the paper.

"What does it say?" she asked.

Arjun's eyes lifted to hers, the shadows in them colder than ice. He handed her the note.

Natasha's breath stilled as her eyes scanned the words.

"Tell her the truth, or we will."

Her hands shook as she lowered the paper. "Who—who wrote this?"

Arjun's gaze sharpened. He didn't answer. Instead, he crossed the room and pulled on his coat.

"Arjun—"

"Get your things," he said, his voice hard.

"Where are we going?"

"Someplace safe."

She hesitated. "And if they find us?"

Arjun's gaze darkened. "They will."

She swallowed. "Then why are we running?"

His eyes flashed as he stepped toward her, closing the space between them. His hands caught her face, his touch rough and desperate.

"Because if they catch you," he whispered, "They won't let you go."

Her breath hitched. He leaned in, his forehead pressing against hers. His breath shuddered against her lips.

"But they won't touch you," he said, voice low and dangerous. "I won't let them."

Her hands slid over his chest, her heart thundering beneath her ribs.

"You're scaring me," she whispered.

His lips brushed the curve of her jaw. His fingers tightened at the back of her neck.

"Good," he said darkly.

And then—

The lights cut out.

Darkness swallowed the room.

Natasha's breath sharpened. Arjun's hand immediately gripped her arm, steady and firm.

A soft sound echoed from the hallway. The sound of footsteps.

Slow. Measured.

Arjun swore under his breath. He grabbed Natasha's hand and pulled her toward the door leading to the back staircase.

"We have to move."

They pushed through the door and into the dark stairwell. The air was thick and cold, the concrete steps slick beneath their feet.

Arjun's grip on her hand was iron tight as they descended.

A noise echoed behind them—soft and deliberate.

Footsteps.

They weren't alone.

Arjun pulled her into the shadow of the wall, his body pressing against hers to keep her hidden. His breath was harsh against her ear.

"We're being followed," he whispered.

Natasha's pulse hammered painfully.

And then—

A voice.

Low. Male. Cold.

"Mr. Arjun," it said, echoing through the stairwell.

Arjun's body tensed against hers.

"You've had enough time," the voice continued. "But now it's her turn."

Natasha's blood chilled.

Arjun's hand slid to her waist, his touch burning through the cold. His mouth brushed against her ear.

"When I say run," he murmured, "you run."

Her breath hitched. "Arjun—"

He pressed his forehead to hers, his hand sliding to her jaw. His lips—soft, yet dangerous—hovered over hers.

"I love you," he whispered.

And then—

A sharp burst of light flooded the stairwell.

Arjun pulled her hand, and they ran.

Natasha's breath burned in her throat as they flew down the steps. The sound of pursuit followed close behind—boots on concrete, sharp and fast.

They reached the bottom, and Arjun shoved open the door to the alley.

Cold rain lashed at them as they stumbled into the dark.

A figure stepped into the light at the far end of the alley.

Black gloves. Hooded.

Arjun's grip tightened on Natasha's hand.

"Arjun…"

"Keep running," he said.

But this time—

The figure stepped forward.

"You can't outrun this," the figure said.

And beneath the hood—

A smile.

A familiar smile.

Natasha's breath froze. "No…"

Arjun's body coiled, ready to fight.

The figure's smile widened.

"You should've stayed dead."

Chapter 21:
Beneath the Rain

The alley was narrow and dark, the rain cascading down the brick walls in cold sheets. Arjun's breath was ragged, his chest rising and falling as his grip on Natasha's hand tightened.

The figure in the hood took a step forward.

"You should've stayed dead."

Arjun's jaw clenched. His arm shot protectively in front of Natasha, pushing her back.

"What you want?" Arjun's voice was low and dangerous.

The figure chuckled softly—a sound that scraped against the damp air. "You already know the answer to that."

Natasha's eyes darted between them, her chest tightening with confusion. She could feel the tension radiating off Arjun—his body poised, coiled like a predator waiting to strike.

"Stop playing games," Arjun growled.

The figure's gloved hand lifted, a slip of paper clutched between his fingers. He held it out toward them.

Natasha's breath hitched.

"Take it," the figure said.

Arjun didn't move.

"Take it," the figure repeated, his voice soft but cutting.

Slowly, Arjun's hand left Natasha's waist. He stepped forward, eyes burning with quiet fury. His fingers brushed the paper as he took it.

Natasha watched as his gaze darkened.

"What is it?" she asked, her voice trembling.

Arjun's hand curled around the paper. His breath sharpened. "It's a name."

The figure smiled beneath the shadow of his hood.

"You have three days, Arjun." His voice was low, dripping with quiet malice. "And then we come for her."

Natasha's heart seized.

Arjun's body went rigid. "If you touch her—"

"You don't have a choice," the figure cut in. "You know how this works."

Arjun's hand shot out, gripping the figure's collar and slamming him against the wall.

Natasha gasped.

"Arjun!"

The figure didn't resist. He laughed—low and dark—as Arjun's arm pressed harder against his throat.

"You're already too late," the figure whispered.

Arjun's fist tightened. "You'll regret this."

The figure's smile widened. "No, Arjun. You will."

Arjun's eyes flashed. His grip tightened—but then, the figure dissolved into shadow, slipping beneath Arjun's hands as though he was made of smoke. He stepped back into the darkness of the alley and vanished.

Natasha ran to Arjun's side, her hands finding his arm.

"What was that?" she breathed.

Arjun's jaw was tight, his breathing shallow. He didn't speak for a moment.

Then, slowly, he opened his hand.

Natasha's gaze dropped to the slip of paper resting in his palm.

A single name was scrawled in ink.

Julian.

Her gaze lifted to Arjun's face. His expression was dark, his eyes lost beneath the shadow of something she didn't understand.

"Who's Julian?" she whispered.

Arjun closed his hand around the paper. "Someone I thought was dead."

Natasha's breath quickened. "And now he's after us?"

Arjun's hand slid to her waist, drawing her closer. His eyes—stormy and burning—locked onto hers.

"No," he said softly. "He's after me."

Natasha swallowed, her heart thundering painfully.

"But why?"

"Because I broke a promise," he murmured. "And now, you're the price."

Her breath hitched.

"But I didn't ask for this," she whispered.

Arjun's hand tightened. His forehead pressed against hers, his body a steady warmth against the cold.

"I know," he said.

Natasha's hands slid to his chest. "Then why?"

His lips brushed her temple, lingering there as his breath shuddered.

"Because loving you was never part of the plan."

Her heart stopped.

"But it happened anyway," he whispered.

Natasha's chest tightened painfully. Her hands curled into his shirt.

"Arjun…"

His eyes burned into hers, heavy with unspoken emotion.

"You need to walk away," he said quietly.

"No."

"I can't protect you."

"Yes, you can."

His jaw tightened. His hands slid down her back, resting at the curve of her waist. His eyes darkened with quiet desperation.

"If you stay," he said, his voice low, "You might not survive this."

Her lips parted. Fear curled through her chest—but beneath it, something stronger.

"I don't care," she whispered.

His eyes searched hers. "You should."

"I don't."

Her hands slid to the back of his neck, her heart pounding so loudly she could barely breathe.

"You said it yourself," she whispered. "If they're already coming for me, it's too late to walk away."

A soft breath escaped him. His fingers threaded into her hair.

"You don't understand how dangerous this is," he said darkly.

Her lips curled into a soft smile. "Then make me understand."

Arjun's gaze sharpened.

And then—

He kissed her.

Hard. Desperate.

Natasha's breath caught as his hands framed her face, his mouth pressing into hers with a quiet intensity that stole the air from her lungs. Her hands curled into his shirt, pulling him closer as his lips moved over hers—slow at first, then deeper, more urgent.

He tasted like rain and quiet desperation.

His hands slid down her back, fingers pressing into the curve of her hips as his mouth opened against hers. Natasha's knees weakened, and Arjun's arm slid around her waist, holding her steady as he pressed her back against the wall.

"I don't know how to protect you from this," he whispered against her lips.

Her hands slipped into his hair.

"Then don't," she breathed. "Just don't let me go."

Arjun's forehead dropped to hers. His breath was ragged. His hands trembled at her sides.

"I'm not strong enough to lose you," he whispered.

"You won't."

His mouth hovered over hers. His eyes were sharp and dark, filled with conflict and quiet fear.

And then—

Another sound echoed from the alley.

A low click.

Arjun's body stiffened. His head snapped toward the sound.

Natasha followed his gaze—

A red laser dot danced across the wall.

"Natasha."

His tone was sharpen, urgent.

He grabbed her hand, pulling her away from the wall just as—

Bang!

The bullet shattered the wall behind them. Dust and brick splintered into the air.

Arjun pulled Natasha into the shadows, his body shielding hers.

"Arjun—"

"Run," he said.

She didn't have time to respond before he pulled her down the alley.

Another shot rang out.

Arjun's arm locked around her waist as they stumbled toward the street.

Behind them, footsteps.

Natasha's heart raced.

"Arjun!"

"I've got you," he growled.

She gripped his hand tightly as they tore through the rain-soaked street. Cold air stung her skin.

And just before they reached the next corner—

A sleek black car pulled up to the curb.

The door opened.

Arjun froze.

A man stepped out. Tall. Sharp features. A smile that didn't reach his eyes.

Julian.

His gaze slid toward Natasha.

"Going somewhere?" Julian asked.

Arjun's arm tightened around her.

"Let her go," Arjun said softly. "This isn't about her."

Julian's eyes sharpened dangerously.

"It is now."

Chapter 22:
Into the Fire

The wind howled around them, whipping Arjun's hair into a wild mess as he stood between Natasha and Julian. His breath was ragged, his jaw tense. Natasha could feel the heat of his body at her side, his arm curling protectively around her waist.

Julian's sharp eyes gleamed beneath the dim glow of the streetlight. He stood beside the sleek black car, his hands tucked casually into his pockets as though this were a friendly meeting between old acquaintances. But there was nothing casual about the look in his eyes—cold, calculating, and dangerous.

"Going somewhere?" Julian's tone was light, conversational, but the weight beneath it was unmistakable.

Arjun's body tensed. His hand slid to Natasha's wrist, his fingers tightening slightly.

"We're leaving," Arjun said, his voice low and controlled.

Julian's smile sharpened. "I'm afraid that's not an option."

Arjun's eyes darkened. "You don't get to tell me what's an option anymore."

Julian chuckled softly. He took a step forward, his gaze slipping toward Natasha. She fought the instinct to shrink away.

"I see you've been busy." Julian's eyes flicked over her, lingering a moment too long.

Arjun's arm tightened around Natasha's waist. His voice dropped to a lethal edge. "Don't."

Julian's smile widened. "Relax. I'm just curious. After all, she's the reason you came back, isn't she?"

Arjun's jaw tightened.

Julian's eyes glinted in the wind-swept darkness. "That's… dangerous."

Natasha's pulse hammered painfully in her throat.

Julian's gaze slid toward Arjun. "You broke the rules."

Arjun's hand curled into a fist at his side. "The rules were broken a long time ago."

Julian's smile thinned. "And yet, here you are."

Arjun took a step forward, placing himself fully between Natasha and Julian.

"I'm not going back," Arjun said, his voice ice-cold.

Julian's smile disappeared. The easy charm in his expression darkened into something colder, more lethal.

"You don't have a choice," Julian said softly.

Natasha's heart seized. She could feel the tension radiating off Arjun's body—the barely restrained violence simmering beneath the surface.

"Take a step closer," Arjun said, his voice dangerously low, "And see what happens."

Julian's gaze sharpened. "You think you can fight this?"

Arjun's hand slid toward his jacket. Natasha's breath hitched as she saw the glint of metal beneath the fabric.

Julian's eyes darkened.

"You haven't changed at all," Julian murmured.

Arjun's jaw clenched. His finger brushed the grip of the gun beneath his jacket.

"I've changed enough."

Julian's smile returned. "We'll see."

Suddenly, there was movement in the shadows behind Julian. Two men stepped out of the darkness, their silhouettes sharp against the wind-swept street. Dressed in black. Armed.

Natasha's breath hitched.

Arjun's hand shot toward his jacket, drawing the gun in a swift motion. He lifted it, his body braced in front of Natasha.

"Stay behind me," he ordered.

Natasha's heart pounded.

Julian's gaze flicked toward the gun. His smile widened slightly. "Careful, Arjun. That's not going to help you."

Arjun's eyes narrowed. "I'm not interested in helping myself."

Julian's gaze sharpened.

"You can't win this," Julian said softly. "You know how this ends."

Arjun's finger tightened on the trigger. "Not tonight."

A single shot echoed through the alley.

Arjun fired, striking one of the men in the shoulder. The man stumbled back with a sharp curse.

Julian's smile vanished. "Very well."

The other man lifted a weapon—

Arjun fired again.

The second man went down, collapsing to his knees with a grunt of pain.

Julian's expression remained cold and untouched.

"Go!" Arjun shouted, grabbing Natasha's arm.

Natasha stumbled as Arjun pulled her toward the opposite end of the alley.

"Arjun—"

"Don't stop!"

They ran, their feet slamming against the wet pavement. Natasha's breath burned in her throat, cold air whipping against her face.

Behind them, Julian's voice echoed through the rain.

"You can't run from this, Arjun!"

Arjun's grip tightened.

They burst out onto the main street, the sharp glow of streetlights illuminating the wet pavement. A car screeched to a stop at the curb.

A dark figure stepped out.

Arjun cursed, pulling Natasha toward the opposite side of the street.

"Come on!"

They darted between the parked cars, their breath ragged and sharp. Arjun's arm was tight around her waist as he guided her through the maze of narrow alleys and back streets.

Finally, Arjun pulled Natasha into a darkened doorway, his hand pressed tightly over her mouth as he leaned them both against the wall.

Her heart was pounding so hard she could barely think.

Arjun's breath was warm against her ear. His body shielded hers completely, his chest rising and falling with the force of his breathing.

"Are they—"

"Shh."

Natasha's breath hitched as Arjun's hand slid from her mouth to her jaw. His thumb brushed her cheek, his other hand pressed to the small of her back.

For a long moment, neither of them moved.

Arjun's forehead dropped to hers, his breath harsh and ragged.

"You okay?" he murmured.

She nodded weakly, her hands clutching his jacket. "What the hell was that?"

Arjun's hands slid to her face, his touch rough but careful.

"That was Julian," he said quietly.

"And those men—"

"His."

Her chest tightened. "What does he want?"

Arjun's eyes darkened. "To finish what we started."

Natasha's hands curled into the fabric of his jacket. Her heart was still racing. Her whole body was trembling.

Arjun's thumb brushed the corner of her mouth, his gaze sharp and fierce. "I need you to listen to me."

She swallowed hard.

"You can't trust anyone now," he said.

Her breath shuddered. "Including you?"

Arjun's eyes softened. His forehead pressed against hers. His breath was warm, steady.

"I will *always* protect you." His voice was rough, dangerous. "But this doesn't end here."

Natasha's heart raced.

Her hands slid up his chest, curling at the back of his neck. His breath hitched as her fingertips brushed his skin.

"Then don't leave me," she whispered.

His eyes burned into hers.

"Never."

He leaned down, his lips brushing against hers. His hands slid down her back, pulling her closer. Natasha's breath caught as his mouth claimed hers—a slow, desperate kiss that tasted like rain and fear and quiet longing.

Arjun's hand slid to the back of her neck, deepening the kiss. Natasha's body melted into his, her hands tightening around his jacket.

When they broke apart, their foreheads touched.

Arjun's breath was ragged. "We need to move."

Natasha nodded, her hands sliding down his chest.

She took his hand.

And this time—

She didn't let go.

Chapter 23:
The Ghosts of Yesterday

The rain had slowed to a soft drizzle by the time they slipped through the back door of a narrow building in the heart of the city. The alley behind them was dark, empty except for the quiet hum of distant traffic and the glint of wet pavement beneath the streetlights.

Arjun's hand was tight around Natasha's wrist as he guided her through the dimly lit hallway. The scent of old wood and damp air clung to the narrow walls. His eyes flicked toward every shadow, his body wound tight with tension.

Natasha's breath was still uneven, her chest rising and falling as adrenaline slowly leaked from her veins. Her hand trembled in Arjun's grip, but she didn't pull away.

Arjun pushed open a door at the end of the hallway and pulled her inside.

A small room. Dim lighting. A leather couch sat beneath a fogged window, and a wooden desk was pushed against the wall. The room smelled faintly of whiskey and dust.

Arjun locked the door behind them and turned toward her. His eyes were sharp and dark.

"Sit," he said.

Natasha hesitated. "Arjun—"

"*Sit.*"

She sank down onto the edge of the couch, her pulse hammering against her throat. Arjun paced toward the window, dragging a hand through his wet hair.

"I need to know what's going on," Natasha said, her voice cutting through the quiet.

Arjun's back tensed. He didn't turn.

"Arjun."

He let out a sharp breath. His hand flattened against the fogged glass. His reflection stared back at him—cold and hard-edged.

"You said the book was a confession," Natasha pressed. "A confession about what?"

Arjun's jaw tightened. He turned slowly, his eyes sharp beneath the low light.

"There's something I didn't tell you," he said.

Her chest tightened. "Then tell me."

Arjun crossed the room in two steps, his hands sliding into the pockets of his jacket. His gaze was intense, locked onto hers.

"You know I left," he said quietly. "After... everything."

"Yes."

"And you know I completed the book afterward."

"Yes."

"What I didn't tell you," Arjun's voice darkened, "Was why."

Natasha's breath caught.

Arjun leaned back against the desk, his eyes narrowing. "It wasn't just a story. It was a map."

Her brow furrowed. "A map?"

Arjun's eyes sharpened. "I didn't make the story up. I recorded it."

Natasha's heart stilled.

Arjun's gaze slid toward the window. His jaw tightened. "I was part of something," he said. "Years ago."

"The society?" Natasha whispered.

Arjun's eyes darkened. "Yes."

Her pulse quickened.

Arjun's hand curled into a fist at his side. His voice dropped, low and edged with quiet intensity.

"They recruited me when I was nineteen. I didn't understand what it was at first—it seemed harmless enough. A group. A brotherhood. But then things started changing."

Her brow furrowed. "What kind of changes?"

Arjun's eyes sharpened. "They started collecting information—personal details about people. Private lives. Relationships. Patterns. I thought it was about security—understanding people better."

Natasha's stomach twisted.

"But it wasn't?"

Arjun shook his head. "It was about control."

Her breath hitched.

"They wanted influence," Arjun said. "To pull strings behind the scenes. To know how people would act before they acted. How to predict outcomes and control them." His jaw flexed. "And they were getting better at it."

Natasha's pulse quickened. "How?"

Arjun's mouth tightened. "Surveillance. Psychological profiling. It started with data—simple patterns in behavior. But then it became personal."

Natasha's breath caught.

"They knew things," Arjun continued. "Things no one should know. Private conversations. Secrets. Weaknesses." His gaze darkened. "And they started using them."

Her chest tightened painfully. "To what end?"

"To manipulate people," Arjun said. "To control outcomes."

Natasha's hands curled into her lap. "And you were helping them?"

Arjun's jaw flexed. "Not intentionally. I thought I was part of something important—something good." His gaze sharpened. "Until I realized what they were really doing."

Her breath quickened.

"I tried to leave," Arjun said quietly. "But they don't like when people walk away."

Her heart hammered painfully. "What did they do?"

"They made sure I understood the consequences," Arjun said darkly. "They reminded me how easy it was to make someone's life… difficult."

Natasha's breath hitched.

"I was a loose thread," Arjun said. "But they didn't cut me off completely. Not yet."

"Why not?"

Arjun's eyes sharpened. "Because I had leverage."

Her pulse spiked.

"What kind of leverage?"

Arjun's gaze darkened. His hands slid into his jacket pockets.

"I took something from them," he said.

Natasha's chest tightened painfully. "What?"

"Proof," Arjun said. "Records of how they operated. The methods they used. The people involved."

Her breath stopped.

"And you put it in the book?"

"Not directly," Arjun said. "But the story—the characters—they match the real system. If you know how to read it, the book tells you how to unravel the whole thing."

Natasha's heart thudded painfully. "So Julian knows you wrote it?"

Arjun nodded. "That's why he's after us."

Her chest tightened painfully. "But why now?"

Arjun's jaw flexed. "Because the book isn't enough. There's a key."

Her breath caught. "What kind of key?"

"A cipher," Arjun said. "It's the only way to decode the information hidden in the book. Without it, the story is meaningless."

Natasha's brow furrowed. "And you don't have it anymore?"

Arjun's gaze sharpened.

"I left it with you," he said softly.

Her breath hitched.

"What?"

"I gave it to you months ago," Arjun said.

Natasha's mind raced. "What are you talking about?"

"The locket," Arjun said quietly.

Her breath stopped. "My mother's locket?"

"Yes."

Natasha's hands trembled as she reached for the delicate chain around her neck. The small silver pendant rested against her palm, cold and familiar.

"I never opened it," she whispered.

"Open it," Arjun said quietly.

Her hands shook as she unclasped the locket.

Inside—

A thin slip of paper, folded tightly.

Her pulse hammered as she carefully unfolded it. A series of letters and symbols scrawled across the paper in Arjun's handwriting.

Her breath caught. "What is this?"

"The cipher," Arjun said.

Natasha's eyes lifted to his. "You hid it with me?"

Arjun's hand slid to her face, his thumb brushing her cheek.

"Because I knew you were the only one I could trust," he whispered.

Her breath shuddered. Her hand curled into his jacket.

"Arjun—"

He leaned in, his forehead pressing against hers.

"And now," he said softly, "we have to use it."

Natasha's breath caught. "And if we don't?"

Arjun's lips brushed against hers, soft and lingering.

"Then they'll take it from you," he whispered.

Her heart slammed painfully against her ribs.

Her hands slid to his neck, her lips parting beneath his.

"We won't let that happen," she whispered.

Arjun's eyes darkened.

"Then let's finish this."

Chapter 24:
Hidden Truths

The paper trembled between Natasha's fingers as the rain continued to patter softly against the window. The symbols and letters on the slip of paper inside the locket blurred beneath her gaze.

"You knew I had this?" Natasha whispered, her breath uneven.

Arjun's eyes darkened. He crouched in front of her, his hands resting lightly on her knees. His touch was grounding—steady despite the storm in his gaze.

"I left it with you for a reason," he said softly.

Natasha's heart thudded painfully. "Why didn't you tell me?"

"Because I didn't want you involved." His thumb brushed her knee, his touch gentle despite the tension beneath his skin. "But it was always going to come to this."

Her breath caught. "Why?"

"Because Julian knows," Arjun said, his gaze sharpening. "And if he finds the key—"

Her pulse spiked. "What happens?"

Arjun's jaw tightened. He stood slowly, his gaze burning into hers.

"If Julian decodes the book," Arjun said, "he'll have control over everything the society built. Every connection. Every influence." His mouth tightened. "And once he has that kind of power, no one will be able to stop him."

Natasha's chest constricted painfully.

"But why does he need *me*?"

"Because you have the key," Arjun said. His gaze softened. "And because he knows I'll do anything to protect you."

Her breath hitched. Her fingers curled tightly around the locket.

"Then we destroy it," she said.

Arjun's gaze sharpened. "It's not that simple."

"Why not?"

Arjun sat beside her on the couch, his hand sliding to the small of her back. His touch was warm despite the chill still clinging to her skin.

"Because the cipher isn't just a code," Arjun said. "It's a map."

Her brow furrowed. "A map to what?"

"To where I hid the final piece."

Natasha's breath stilled.

"You hid it?"

Arjun's mouth curled faintly. "Of course."

Her heart pounded. "And now we have to find it?"

Arjun's gaze darkened. "Before Julian does."

The paper in her hand crinkled slightly beneath her fingers. She unfolded it again, scanning the symbols and letters.

"What does it mean?" she asked.

Arjun leaned in, his hand brushing against hers as he studied the paper. His brow furrowed slightly.

"It's a combination," he said. "Numbers and letters tied to specific locations."

"Locations?"

He nodded. "Places connected to the society."

Her breath caught. "And you think Julian knows?"

Arjun's jaw flexed. "He knows enough."

Natasha's pulse hammered painfully.

"So where do we start?"

Arjun's hand slid to hers, his fingers curling over her trembling ones.

"There's one place I didn't put in the book," he said. "One place Julian wouldn't think to check."

"Where?"

Arjun's gaze sharpened.

"My father's house."

Natasha's breath stopped.

"But I thought—"

"He left it to me before he disappeared," Arjun said quietly. His jaw tightened. "I haven't been back since."

Her heart raced.

"Arjun…"

He stood, pulling her up with him. His hands slid to her waist, steady despite the storm behind his eyes.

"It's the only place left," he said softly.

Her hand slid up his chest, her fingers curling into the fabric of his shirt.

"Then let's go," she whispered.

Arjun's eyes flashed. His hands tightened around her waist.

"You're not scared?"

Her lips curled slightly. "Terrified."

His mouth twitched. His thumb brushed the side of her jaw.

"Then why are you still standing here?"

Her breath hitched. Her hands slid to his collar, pulling him down until his lips hovered just above hers.

"Because I trust you," she whispered.

Arjun's breath sharpened. His forehead pressed to hers. His lips brushed against her mouth—soft and lingering.

"Then we don't have time to waste," he said.

Natasha's heart slammed painfully against her ribs as Arjun's hand slid into hers, pulling her toward the door.

Two Hours Later

The road leading to Arjun's father's house was dark and narrow, lined with thick trees that leaned toward the road like shadows reaching for them. The rain had stopped, but the air was heavy with moisture.

Natasha's hand rested on her thigh as Arjun drove, his gaze sharp and focused on the winding road ahead.

The house came into view at the top of a narrow hill.

It was old—three stories of dark wood and sloping rooftops, surrounded by a black iron gate. The windows were dark, and the overgrown ivy clinging to the exterior made the house look almost haunted.

Arjun pulled the car to stop outside the gate. He killed the engine and sat back, his hand still resting on the wheel.

"You sure about this?" Natasha asked.

Arjun's gaze flicked toward her. "No."

Her chest tightened.

"But we don't have a choice," he added.

Arjun stepped out of the car, the cool night air pressing against them. Natasha followed, her breath fogging slightly in the chill.

Arjun approached the gate, sliding his hand beneath the iron frame. A soft click echoed through the night, and the gate creaked open.

"How do you know it's not already compromised?" Natasha whispered.

"I don't," Arjun said.

Her heart hammered as they stepped through the gate.

Arjun led her up the stone path toward the front door. His hand slid to the small of her back, guiding her.

He reached for the lock beneath the handle—and the door opened beneath his touch.

Natasha's breath sharpened.

"It's open," she whispered.

Arjun's gaze darkened. "I noticed."

They stepped inside.

The house was dark and cold. The scent of dust and old wood clung to the air. Moonlight filtered through the large bay windows, casting long shadows across the hardwood floors.

Natasha's pulse quickened.

"Where are we going?" she whispered.

Arjun's hand slid to hers. His grip was steady.

"Upstairs," he said.

They moved down the hallway, their footsteps soft against the wood.

At the top of the stairs, Arjun stopped. His gaze sharpened.

"Here," he said quietly.

He pressed his hand against the wall beside the door. There was a soft click, and the panel slid open, revealing a small hidden compartment.

Arjun reached inside. His hand curled around a thin leather-bound notebook.

He pulled it free and handed it to Natasha.

Her fingers slid over the leather. The edges were worn, the spine creased.

"What is it?"

"The original code," Arjun said. "The one I based the book on."

Her breath hitched.

"You wrote this?"

Arjun's mouth curved faintly. "Not all of it."

Her pulse quickened. "Then who did?"

His gaze sharpened.

"My father."

Her chest constricted.

Natasha flipped open the notebook, her fingers brushing the pages.

Symbols. Letters. Maps. All tied together with careful notes in Arjun's handwriting.

"This is everything?" she whispered.

"Yes."

Her eyes lifted to his. "And Julian knows?"

Arjun's jaw flexed. "He suspects."

Natasha's breath hitched. "So what do we do now?"

Arjun's hand slid to her face. His thumb brushed her lower lip.

"Now," he said softly, "we finish this."

Her pulse hammered painfully.

"And if Julian finds us first?"

Arjun's lips brushed against hers.

"Then we make sure he regrets it."

Chapter 25:
No Turning Back

The air inside the house was thick with silence. Dust hung in the cold moonlight streaming through the tall windows, illuminating the edges of the dark hardwood floor.

Natasha's heart hammered painfully beneath her ribs as she stood beside Arjun in the hallway. Her fingers curled around the worn leather notebook he'd just handed her. The symbols and letters on the pages blurred beneath the flickering light of the hallway sconce.

Her breath trembled as Arjun's hand slid to the small of her back. His touch was warm despite the chill in the air.

"We have what we need," Arjun said, his voice low.

Natasha's eyes lifted to his face. His gaze was sharp, cutting through the dim light. His body was wound tight, tension radiating off him like static.

"But we don't know what it means yet," Natasha said.

Arjun's hand slid down to her wrist, his thumb brushing over her pulse. "We'll figure it out."

Natasha's chest tightened. "And if Julian finds us first?"

Arjun's jaw flexed. His gaze darkened.

"He won't."

Her pulse quickened beneath his touch.

"How can you be so sure?" she whispered.

Arjun's hand slid to the side of her face, his thumb brushing the curve of her jaw. His breath ghosted over her lips as he leaned in.

"Because I'm not letting him near you," he said, his voice low and sharp.

Her breath hitched.

Arjun's eyes searched hers, dark and stormy. His thumb traced the curve of her cheek, and his hand slid to the back of her neck.

Her heart pounded so hard it ached.

"You keep saying that," Natasha whispered.

"Because I mean it."

Her lips parted. Arjun's mouth hovered inches from hers, his breath warm and unsteady.

"You don't need to protect me," Natasha said softly.

Arjun's gaze sharpened. His fingers tightened at her nape.

"I do," he said darkly. "Because I already lost you once."

Her breath caught.

"And I'm not losing you again."

Natasha's chest squeezed painfully. Her hands slid up his chest, her fingertips brushing over the thin fabric of his shirt.

"You didn't lose me," she whispered.

Arjun's breath hitched. His forehead pressed against hers.

"You don't understand," he said softly. "Julian—he'll do whatever it takes."

Natasha's hands curled into his shirt. Her pulse thundered against her throat.

"Then let him try," she said.

Arjun's gaze sharpened.

Natasha leaned into him, her lips brushing against his jaw. Her breath shuddered over his skin.

"You're not alone anymore," she whispered.

Arjun's chest tightened beneath her hands.

His mouth hovered just over hers. His hand curled around the back of her neck, his fingers threading through her hair.

"You're playing with fire," he said, his voice rough.

Natasha's lips curled faintly. "Good."

And then—

Arjun kissed her.

Hard. Desperate.

Natasha's breath vanished as his mouth claimed hers, his hands sliding down her back. Her fingers curled into his shirt, pulling him closer as his lips moved over hers—deep and searching.

Arjun's hand slid to her waist, pressing her back against the wall. His mouth was hot and rough, his breath ragged against her skin.

Natasha's arms slid around his neck. Her body melted into his as his mouth claimed hers again, more demanding this time.

"Arjun," she gasped.

He pulled back, his forehead pressed against hers, his breath heavy. His hands cupped her face, his eyes dark and burning.

"I'm not letting you go," he said, his voice low and dangerous.

Natasha's breath trembled.

"I don't want you to," she whispered.

Arjun's mouth brushed over hers again—softer this time. His hands slid down her arms, anchoring her to him.

"I don't know how to keep you safe," he whispered.

Her lips parted.

"Then stop trying," she said.

Arjun's breath hitched.

Her hand slid up to his face, her thumb brushing over his cheekbone. His eyes burned into hers—dark and guarded and full of quiet desperation.

"I'm not running," Natasha whispered.

Arjun's chest heaved beneath her hand. His eyes softened.

"I know."

Her hands curled into the back of his neck, her breath brushing against his mouth.

"So stop pushing me away," she said.

Arjun's mouth curled faintly. His hands slid down her waist, pulling her closer.

"Dangerous words," he said.

Her lips brushed against his.

"I'm done being careful."

Arjun's mouth curved into a dark smile.

"Good," he whispered.

And then he kissed her again.

Natasha's hands slid into his hair as his mouth deepened against hers. His hands pressed into the small of her back, pulling her closer until their bodies molded together.

Her breath hitched as his lips trailed down the curve of her jaw, his breath hot against her skin. His hands slid to her hips, his thumb brushing beneath the hem of her sweater.

"Arjun," she breathed.

His mouth hovered just over hers. His gaze was sharp and dark.

"Say it again," he murmured.

Her chest tightened. "Arjun."

A flicker of something softer—something vulnerable—flashed behind his eyes. His mouth brushed over hers again, slower this time.

"I can't lose you," he whispered.

"You won't."

His hand slid to her jaw, his thumb brushing the edge of her mouth. His gaze sharpened.

"I mean it," he said softly.

"So do I."

Arjun's breath stilled. His eyes darkened.

Natasha's hands slid down his chest.

"We're in this together," she whispered.

His mouth curled faintly. "Together?"

She smiled softly. "Always."

Arjun's gaze burned into hers. His hand slid through her hair, anchoring her to him.

"Then we don't stop," he said.

Her breath quickened.

"Not until this is finished."

Natasha's hand slid to his wrist, her fingers curling over the edge of his jacket.

"Where do we start?"

Arjun's mouth curved into a dark smile.

"We follow the map."

Her breath hitched.

"And if Julian catches up?" she whispered.

Arjun's thumb brushed over her lower lip. His gaze sharpened.

"Then we make sure he regrets it."

Natasha's heart hammered.

Arjun's hand slid to her back. His mouth hovered just over hers.

"And until then," he whispered, "You're mine."

Her breath stilled.

"And you're mine," she whispered.

Arjun's mouth curled into a faint smile.

"Then let's see how far we can push them."

Chapter 26:
Betrayal in the Dark

The morning sun filtered weakly through the tall bay windows, casting pale light across the room. Dust floated in the beams, disturbed only by the faint sound of Natasha's breath as she sat cross-legged on the floor beside Arjun.

The notebook lay open between them, its worn leather edges curling at the corners. Pages filled with symbols, coordinates, and patterns lay beneath Arjun's fingertips as he traced the markings with quiet focus.

Natasha watched him, her pulse steady but elevated. His dark eyes flicked over the pages, calculating and dissecting. A muscle flexed in his jaw as he studied the symbols.

"This is more complicated than I remember," Arjun muttered.

Natasha leaned in closer. "What are you seeing?"

Arjun's brow furrowed. His finger stopped over a cluster of symbols etched carefully in the margins.

"Patterns," he said. "Repeated sequences."

Natasha studied the symbols. Circles, lines, and letters connected by sharp angles. Some were crossed out, others underlined.

"It looks like coordinates," Natasha said.

Arjun's gaze sharpened. "It is."

Her chest tightened. "To where?"

Arjun's lips curled faintly. "That's the question."

Natasha's eyes scanned the page. Her fingertips brushed the edge of the paper. "How do we figure it out?"

Arjun exhaled slowly. His hand slid to the back of his neck, his eyes narrowing.

"There's a pattern here, but it's layered," he said. "Whoever wrote this didn't want it solved easily."

Natasha's gaze flicked toward him. "Your father?"

Arjun's mouth tightened.

"Yes."

Her heart stilled. "You think he left this for you?"

Arjun's gaze darkened. "Not for me. For someone who could finish what he started."

Natasha's pulse quickened. "What did he start?"

Arjun's hand curled into a fist. His gaze sharpened.

"My father wasn't just part of the society," Arjun said quietly. "He helped build it."

Natasha's breath hitched.

"What?"

Arjun's mouth curled bitterly. "He designed the system. The codes. The infrastructure. All of it."

Her pulse hammered painfully.

"But why?"

Arjun's eyes darkened. "Because he believed in it."

Natasha's heart constricted.

"But you don't?"

Arjun's gaze flashed. "Not anymore."

Natasha's fingers curled into her lap. "What changed?"

Arjun hesitated. His jaw tightened.

"My father left," Arjun said finally. His gaze was sharp and hollow. "He walked away from everything."

Natasha's brow furrowed. "Why?"

"Because he realized it wasn't about helping people anymore," Arjun said darkly. "It was about control."

Her breath caught.

"And when he left," Arjun's mouth twisted, "He made sure they couldn't replicate what he built."

Natasha's heart thudded painfully.

"You mean this code."

Arjun nodded. His hand slid down the page, his finger stopping at a cluster of symbols beneath a sketched line.

"He encrypted it," Arjun said. "Buried the key beneath layers of false patterns."

"So how do we unlock it?" Natasha asked.

Arjun's gaze darkened. "We follow the trail."

Her pulse quickened. "What trail?"

Arjun lifted the notebook, holding it toward her. His finger tapped beneath the symbol at the top of the page.

"This symbol," he said.

Natasha studied it—a circle intersected by a triangle.

"It's a marker," Arjun said. "A location."

Her breath caught. "Where?"

Arjun's mouth curved faintly. "The museum."

Natasha's brows lifted. "The museum?"

Arjun nodded. "My father helped design the security system there. If he left something behind, it'll be hidden where only someone who understands his work could find it."

Natasha's chest tightened.

"And you think Julian knows?"

Arjun's gaze sharpened.

"If he doesn't already," Arjun said, "he will soon."

Natasha's hands curled into her lap. Her pulse hammered painfully.

"Then we don't have much time," she said.

Arjun's gaze sharpened. His mouth curled faintly.

"No."

He stood, holding out his hand.

"Come on," he said.

Natasha's gasped. Her hand slid into his. His fingers curled over hers, warm and steady.

"We find it first," Arjun said.

Natasha stood, her chest tightening beneath the weight of his gaze.

"And if Julian's there?"

Arjun's eyes darkened. His jaw tightened.

"Then we improvise."

The Museum

The museum's marble steps were slick beneath Natasha's boots as they climbed toward the entrance beneath the dark canopy of night.

The towering columns loomed above them, casting long shadows against the stone facade. The entrance was flanked by two large sculptures—winged figures carved in pale stone.

Arjun's hand tightened over Natasha's as they approached the side entrance.

"How do you know the code still works?" Natasha whispered.

Arjun smiled faintly. "My father wasn't the kind of man to leave loose ends."

Her pulse quickened.

Arjun slid a small keycard from his jacket and pressed it against the scanner beside the door.

The lock clicked open.

"Still works," Arjun said softly.

They slipped inside.

The museum's darkened halls stretched out before them, lined with marble columns and glass cases containing centuries-old artifacts. Their footsteps echoed softly against the polished floor.

Arjun's gaze flicked toward the ceiling. A small red light blinked above the archway.

"Security cameras?" Natasha whispered.

"Disabled," Arjun said.

Natasha's brows lifted. "You're sure?"

Arjun's mouth curved faintly.

"Not entirely."

Her pulse hammered.

They moved down the hall, their footsteps light against the stone. Arjun's hand slid to the small of her back, guiding her toward a narrow side door.

He stopped at the threshold.

"Here," he said.

Natasha's breath quickened.

"What's in there?"

Arjun's gaze darkened.

"My father's office."

Her chest tightened.

Arjun pressed his hand to the panel beside the door. It slid open with a soft hiss.

The office was dark. Dust motes floated in the pale light filtering through the high windows. Shelves lined the walls—rows of old books and files stacked beneath glass cases.

Arjun moved toward the desk in the center of the room. His hand slid beneath the edge of the wood.

A soft click echoed through the room.

A hidden drawer slid open beneath the desk.

Natasha's breath sharpened.

Arjun reached inside and pulled free a small leather box. He set it on the desk and flipped open the lid.

Inside—

A thin strip of paper.

Natasha's pulse hammered painfully as Arjun lifted the paper. Symbols and numbers marked the surface in thin black ink.

"What is it?" Natasha asked.

Arjun's gaze sharpened.

"The last piece," he said.

Natasha's breath caught.

Arjun's eyes lifted toward hers, dark and sharp.

"We're done," he said.

Her chest squeezed painfully.

And that's when Natasha's pulse steadied.

Her gaze lowered to the paper in Arjun's hand.

A quiet, calculated calm settled over her.

Her hand slid into the pocket of her jacket and closed around her phone. Her thumb hovered over the screen.

A single message already written.

It's done.

She didn't send it yet.

Arjun's hand brushed her arm. His gaze was steady, trusting.

"I knew we could figure it out," he said softly.

Her chest constricted. Her thumb hovered over the screen for a long, painful second.

And then—

She deleted the message.

Arjun's eyes softened. "Natasha?"

Her smile was thin.

"Let's get out of here," she said.

Chapter 27:
Secrets in the Dark

Natasha's hand slipped out of Arjun's as they walked out of the museum. Her heart hammered painfully against her chest, but her face remained composed—calm even. Years of training made it easy to mask the storm beneath her skin.

Arjun walked ahead of her, his hand wrapped around the thin strip of paper he had taken from the hidden drawer in his father's office. His brow was furrowed, his jaw was tight with quiet determination.

The street was quiet, shrouded in a heavy mist. The glow of the streetlights blurred against the fog, casting soft halos of light over the slick pavement.

Arjun's pace slowed as they reached the edge of the sidewalk.

"We should head back," he said. His voice was low, steady.

Natasha's pulse quickened.

"Arjun," she said softly.

He turned toward her, his dark eyes searching her face.

"What is it?"

Her breath hitched. For a moment, she considered telling him the truth—laying it all bare. But the words caught at the edge of her throat and refused to come out.

Because the truth would ruin him.

And she wasn't ready for that yet.

"We need to figure out what the code means," she said instead.

Arjun's gaze sharpened. "We will."

He lifted the slip of paper between them. His thumb traced the symbols etched in thin black ink.

"I think this is a key," he said. "But it's incomplete."

Natasha's pulse quickened.

"Incomplete?"

Arjun nodded. "There's a missing piece." His gaze darkened. "And I think I know where it is."

Her chest tightened.

"Where?"

Arjun's mouth curled faintly. "The house."

Natasha's blood chilled.

"You mean—"

"My father's house," Arjun said darkly. "He built the foundation of this society there. If he left a final piece, that's where it will be."

Natasha's breath sharpened.

"And Julian?"

Arjun's gaze darkened.

"He'll be there."

Her chest squeezed painfully.

"Arjun—"

"We can't afford to wait anymore," he said, cutting her off. His hand slid to her waist. His eyes softened. "We end this."

Natasha's breath caught as his thumb brushed her jawline. His gaze was steady—trusting.

Her heart twisted painfully.

"Arjun…"

His mouth hovered just above hers. His hands slid to her back, his grip steady and warm.

"I trust you," he whispered.

Her heart cracked beneath the weight of those words.

Her hands curled into his jacket. Her breath hitched painfully.

But Arjun didn't see the conflict behind her eyes. He didn't feel the hesitation beneath her touch.

Because she had been trained not to let him.

She leaned into him, her forehead pressing against his. His breath was steady against her lips. His arms tightened around her waist.

"I need you," he whispered.

Her chest constricted painfully.

And you deserve better.

Natasha's hand slid up his chest. Her fingers curled against the back of his neck. Her mouth brushed over his in a soft, lingering kiss.

Arjun's breath hitched beneath her touch. His hands tightened on her waist, pulling her closer.

But then—

Her phone buzzed in her pocket.

Natasha froze.

Arjun's mouth stilled against hers. His brow furrowed slightly as he leaned back.

"What is it?"

Natasha's breath trembled. Her hand slid toward her jacket pocket.

She already knew what the message would say.

Her eyes dropped to the screen.

A single text.

End it tonight.

Her chest tightened painfully.

"Who is it?" Arjun asked.

Natasha's eyes lifted toward his. His gaze was open—unguarded.

And that made it worse.

"No one," she whispered, slipping the phone back into her pocket.

Arjun's gaze sharpened. "You sure?"

Natasha forced a soft smile. "Yeah."

But her hands were trembling.

And Arjun noticed.

Arjun's Father's House

The house loomed ahead of them like a dark silhouette against the fog. Its sharp edges were softened by the haze, but the cold weight of it pressed against Natasha's chest.

Arjun's hand slid to her back as they stepped through the front gate. The iron gate squealed softly beneath his touch.

The path leading to the front door was cracked and uneven. Ivy curled up the side of the building, twisting around the black windows like veins beneath the skin.

Arjun stopped at the edge of the front steps. His jaw tightened.

"You okay?" Natasha asked softly.

Arjun's gaze sharpened. "This place has always felt haunted."

Natasha's chest squeezed. "Then why come back?"

"Because this is where it ends," Arjun said.

He slid his hand toward the front door. His palm pressed against the wood, and the lock released with a soft click.

The door creaked open.

Arjun's breath sharpened. He stepped inside first, his shoulders tense as his gaze swept the darkened hallway.

Natasha followed, her steps soft against the hardwood floor.

The house was cold. Quiet.

Dust floated through the thin light streaming from the high windows above the staircase.

Arjun's hand brushed over the edge of the banister. His gaze flicked toward the hallway at the end of the stairs.

"Come on," he said.

Natasha's heart thudded painfully as she followed him down the hall.

Arjun stopped at a door near the end of the hallway. His hand slid toward the handle.

"You ready?"

Natasha's mouth curled faintly. "Always."

Arjun pushed open the door.

The room was dark. Shelves lined the walls—rows of old books and files. A large oak desk sat in the center of the room.

Arjun stepped toward the desk, his hand brushing over the edge. He pulled open the drawer beneath it and reached inside.

Natasha's breath hitched as he pulled free a thin leather envelope.

"What is it?" Natasha whispered.

Arjun opened the envelope.

Inside was a single piece of paper.

Marked with symbols.

And a name.

Julian.

Arjun's gaze sharpened. "He knew."

Natasha's chest tightened.

Arjun's eyes lifted toward hers. His gaze darkened. "He knew my father would try to stop him."

Her breath hitched painfully.

Arjun's jaw flexed. "We can end this now."

Natasha's pulse quickened.

But then—

A sound echoed from the hallway.

Footsteps.

Arjun's body tensed. His hand slid toward the paper, slipping it back into the envelope.

"Stay behind me," he said.

Natasha's heart hammered painfully.

And that's when she made her choice.

Her hand slid toward her jacket pocket.

Arjun's eyes sharpened.

"Natasha?"

Her breath caught.

"I'm sorry," she whispered.

Arjun's brow furrowed. "What—"

And then—

Natasha's hand closed around the handle of the door.

She pulled it shut.

Arjun's eyes widened.

"Natasha?"

Her breath hitched.

"I never meant to stay," she whispered.

Arjun's hand shot toward the door handle—

But the lock clicked into place.

"Natasha!"

Tears burned at the edge of her vision as she turned toward the hallway.

She pressed her hand to her mouth, swallowing the sharp sob rising in her throat.

And then—

Her phone buzzed.

A single message.

Good work. Now finish it.

Her breath trembled.

"I'm sorry," Natasha whispered.

And then—

She walked away.

Chapter 28:
Shattered Trust

The hallway was cold and silent, except for the sharp echo of Natasha's heels against the marble floor. Her breath hitched as she moved through the dark corridor, her pulse hammering painfully in her throat.

The sound of Arjun's voice behind the locked door still rang in her ears.

"Natasha!"

His voice had been raw, sharp with confusion and betrayal.

And she had locked him inside.

Her hand trembled as she pressed her palm to the wall, steadying herself. Her chest heaved beneath the thin layer of her jacket.

Her phone buzzed again.

Natasha's breath sharpened as she pulled it from her pocket.

Julian: *Good work. Bring it to me.*

Her heart twisted painfully.

Her fingers curled tightly around the phone. For a moment, she considered ignoring the message. Turning around. Going back to Arjun.

But there was no going back now.

She had crossed the line.

And Arjun—

He would never forgive her for this.

Her hand slid toward her pocket, her fingertips brushing over the outline of the thin leather envelope tucked inside.

The last piece of the code.

Arjun had trusted her with it. He had trusted *her*.

And she had stolen it from him.

Her chest squeezed painfully as she stepped toward the narrow staircase at the end of the hall. Her hand brushed over the banister as she descended into the darkness, her pulse thudding beneath her skin.

The heavy oak door at the bottom of the stairs creaked open beneath her touch.

And Julian was waiting for her.

He stood near the edge of the room, beneath the sharp glow of a single hanging light. His dark suit was perfectly tailored, his mouth curled faintly into a knowing smile.

"Well done," Julian said softly. His gaze slid toward her, cold and sharp. "You've always been reliable."

Natasha's chest tightened again.

She pulled the envelope from her jacket and held it out toward him.

Julian's smile widened as he stepped forward. His long fingers curled over the edge of the envelope, brushing against her hand as he took it from her grasp.

"You have no idea how long I've waited for this," Julian said.

Natasha's breath hitched.

Julian slid the envelope open. His gaze darkened as his eyes scanned the code etched across the paper. His mouth curled faintly.

"Perfect," he murmured.

Natasha's pulse quickened.

"So it's done?" She asked quietly.

Julian's gaze lifted toward hers. His smile faded.

"No," he said softly. "Not yet."

Her breath stilled. "What are you talking about?"

Julian's eyes sharpened.

"You've done well," he said. "But you know how this ends."

Natasha's chest constricted painfully.

"What do you mean?"

Julian stepped closer. His hand slid toward her jaw, his thumb brushing against the curve of her cheek. His touch was cold.

"Loose ends," Julian said softly. "You know how I handle them."

Her breath hitched.

"Julian—"

"I can't have him coming after me," Julian said darkly.

Her eyes widened.

"No," Natasha said sharply. "That wasn't part of the plan."

Julian's smile sharpened.

"You knew what you were doing," he said.

Her pulse spiked painfully.

"You said he wouldn't be hurt," Natasha whispered.

Julian's brow lifted.

"I lied," he said simply.

Her breath caught.

"Julian—"

"Step aside," Julian said.

Her chest tightened. Her hand shot toward his wrist, catching him before he could move toward the door.

"No," Natasha said fiercely.

Julian's eyes darkened.

"Don't make this difficult," Julian said quietly.

Natasha's jaw tightened. Her pulse hammered painfully in her throat.

"I'll handle him," she said.

Julian's gaze sharpened.

"You?"

Natasha's mouth tightened.

"Yes."

Julian's smile faded.

"You care about him," Julian said softly.

Natasha's breath hitched. Her throat tightened painfully.

"I'm the one who brought him into this," she whispered. "I'm the one who finishes it."

Julian's gaze darkened.

"If you don't—"

"I will," Natasha cut in.

Her hand slid toward her pocket. Her fingers curled over the cool weight of the small gun tucked beneath the fabric of her jacket.

Julian's eyes sharpened.

"Prove it," Julian said softly.

Natasha's breath stilled.

Her hand slid toward the door handle.

Her heart hammered painfully.

Arjun's voice echoed faintly through the thin wood.

"Natasha."

Her chest squeezed painfully.

She pressed her hand to the door.

"I'll handle it," she whispered.

Julian's mouth curved faintly.

"You have until midnight."

Natasha's breath sharpened.

"Or I finish it myself," Julian said.

Her hand curled into a fist at her side.

She turned toward the door. Her fingers slid toward the lock.

Her breath hitched painfully as she opened the door.

Arjun stumbled forward, his breath sharp. His dark eyes widened as he caught himself against the frame.

His gaze shot toward hers.

"Natasha?" His voice was rough, sharp with quiet disbelief.

Her breath trembled.

"I'm sorry," she whispered.

Arjun's eyes sharpened. "What—"

She lifted the gun.

Arjun's breath stilled.

"Natasha," he said quietly.

Her hand trembled beneath the weight of the gun. Her pulse hammered painfully beneath her skin.

"I need you to leave," Natasha whispered.

Arjun's jaw tightened. His dark eyes burned into hers.

"You don't have to do this," he said softly.

Her breath hitched painfully.

"Yes, I do."

Arjun's hand lifted toward hers. His fingertips brushed against the curve of her wrist.

"You lied to me," Arjun whispered, his eyes dark with quiet devastation.

Natasha's throat tightened painfully.

"I know," she said softly.

Arjun's hand curled over her wrist. His grip was desperate, shaking.

"I trusted you," he said, his voice rough with betrayal. "You made me believe you cared."

Her breath hitched.

"I did," she whispered.

Arjun's eyes sharpened. His hand slipped away from hers, falling uselessly to his side.

"No," he said darkly. "If you cared, you wouldn't have done this."

Natasha's hand trembled over the gun.

"I had no choice."

"There's always a choice," Arjun said bitterly. "But you chose him."

Her heart twisted painfully.

"I'm sorry," she whispered.

Arjun's eyes burned into hers, his gaze hollowing with the weight of realization.

"You played me," he said, his voice cutting like glass. "From the start."

Her breath sharpened.

Tears burned her eyes.

"I never meant to—"

"Stop," Arjun said coldly. "Just stop."

Natasha's chest squeezed painfully.

"I have to go."

Arjun's jaw tightened. His eyes were dark, glassy.

"You don't get to walk away from this," he said.

"I already have," Natasha whispered.

And then—

She pulled the trigger.

The bullet struck the wall behind him.

Arjun's breath hitched, his eyes widening.

Natasha's hand trembled as his gaze burned into hers, full of disbelief and agony.

"You never loved me," he said, his voice breaking.

Her heart shattered.

"I'm sorry," she whispered.

Arjun's chest rose and fell sharply. His hand curled into a fist at his side.

"You broke me," he whispered.

Natasha's breath hitched painfully.

"I know."

And then—

She walked away.

Chapter 29:

Hollow

Arjun stood in the dark hallway long after Natasha had disappeared.

His breath came sharp and uneven, his chest heaving painfully. His hand was still outstretched where he had reached for her — where he had begged her to stay.

But she had walked away.

His legs felt heavy beneath him as he stumbled forward, pressing his palm to the cold marble wall. His pulse hammered painfully in his ears, drowning out the silence that had settled over the empty corridor.

You lied to me.

Her words echoed through his head like a death knell.

She had never loved him.

She had used him.

And he had let her.

Arjun's hands curled into fists at his sides, his breath ragged as a sharp wave of nausea coiled low in his stomach. His knees buckled, and he sank to the floor, his back pressing against the wall as his chest squeezed painfully tight.

His fingers lifted toward his mouth, brushing over the place where her lips had been. Where her whispered promises had stained his skin.

It was all a lie.

His head tipped back against the wall. His throat burned, his breath shaky.

He had trusted her. Let her in.

And she had stolen everything from him.

A bitter laugh slipped from his throat — thin and broken — before dissolving into silence.

His eyes burned, but no tears fell. His chest was hollow, carved out from the inside.

He closed his eyes. The memory of her touch ghosted over his skin, the scent of her lingering in the air.

Why did it still feel real?

He stayed there for hours — maybe longer — the weight of emptiness pressing down on him until his limbs felt numb.

Eventually, he forced himself to stand. His movements were slow and mechanical as he pushed himself upright, his palm dragging down the length of his face.

He caught a glimpse of himself in the dark glass of the hallway window — pale, hollow-eyed, wrecked. His reflection stared back at him, someone unrecognizable.

You broke me, he had said to her.

And she had.

His hands curled into fists. He had given her everything. His trust. His loyalty. His heart.

And she had crushed it beneath her heel without a second thought.

Arjun's jaw tightened. His breath scraped sharply in his throat as he turned away from the window.

He couldn't feel anything anymore.

Not anger. Not pain. Not hope.

Just… emptiness.

His footsteps were soundless as he walked toward the door. His chest was tight, his breath shallow.

He didn't know where he was going. He didn't care.

He wasn't sure he would ever care again.

Epilogue

Arjun sat alone beneath the soft, dim glow of the city lights.

The night outside his window stretched endlessly, broken only by the distant flicker of headlights cutting through the rain. Water traced slow patterns down the glass, catching the faint shimmer of the streetlights below.

He couldn't remember how long he'd been sitting there — maybe hours, maybe days.

Time had blurred. Stretched. Faded.

His reflection in the glass was hollow — dark eyes rimmed with exhaustion, his jaw tight beneath the faint shadow of unshaven stubble. His hair was tousled and unkempt, falling over his forehead.

He didn't bother to push it back.

The glass felt cold beneath his fingertips as he traced his fingers along the windowpane. His breath fogged faintly against the glass, dissipating almost instantly.

Natasha's face lingered in the quiet.

The soft curl of her smile. The warmth of her laugh. The way her fingers had curled over his wrist when she thought he wasn't paying attention. The light in her eyes when she kissed him.

All of it was a lie.

He knew that now. He had felt the sharp cut of her betrayal beneath his skin — the cold press of the gun against his chest, the finality in her eyes when she told him goodbye.

Still, he couldn't stop seeing her. Hearing her. Feeling her.

The ache sat heavy in his chest, pressing down until it was hard to breathe.

A sharp breeze stirred through the crack in the window. Rain pattered softly against the glass.

Arjun's hand curled into a fist against his knee.

He had been so *stupid*. So blind.

He should have seen it coming. He should have known.

But he had let her in.

He had trusted her.

His head tipped back against the edge of the chair, his eyes burning as he stared at the ceiling. His breath scraped painfully through his throat.

Why did it still hurt so much?

His phone buzzed faintly on the table beside him.

He ignored it.

The calls had been piling up for days — Rehan, his father, even Anaya had called once or twice. They wanted to check on him. They wanted him to talk.

But there was nothing left to say.

He didn't want to explain how it felt to have the ground ripped out from beneath him. To know that the person he had trusted most — the person he had loved — had played him.

Had broken him.

Arjun rubbed the heel of his palm over his chest. The ache beneath his ribs wouldn't go away.

A part of him hated himself for still wanting her.

For missing her.

For loving her despite it all.

His chest rose and fell in shallow, uneven breaths.

He should hate her.

He wanted to hate her.

But all he could feel was the hollow ache where she used to be.

Rain streaked down the window in thin rivulets, blurring the distant glow of the city lights.

His mind drifted back to the last time he had seen her — the weight of the gun in her hand, the tremble in her breath. The quiet resignation in her eyes.

She had known exactly what she was doing.

And she had done it anyway.

His eyes squeezed shut.

He could still feel the ghost of her touch beneath his skin — the press of her hand against his chest, the warmth of her breath against his ear.

"*You broke me,*" he had told her.

And she had.

Completely.

His hands curled into fists. His chest tightened beneath the weight of it.

She had stolen more than the code.

She had stolen *him*.

And now —

He wasn't sure what was left.

Arjun rose slowly from the chair. His footsteps were soundless as he crossed toward the window, his palm flattening against the cool glass. His breath fogged faintly across the surface.

The city stretched out beneath him — restless and bright. Life moved on down there. Cars passed. People walked beneath umbrellas, laughing beneath the glow of the streetlights.

None of it touched him.

His eyes darkened as his gaze settled on the empty horizon.

This — this emptiness — this was what she had left him with.

A hollow shell.

A quiet kind of nothingness.

Arjun's hand slid away from the glass. His chest tightened painfully as he closed his eyes.

For a long time, he stood there — still and silent.

Then —

He turned away from the window.

The shadows stretched long across the floor beneath his feet as he crossed toward the bedroom. His hands slid into the pockets of his jacket. His breath steadied.

No one could hurt him now.

Not anymore.

Because there was nothing left to break.

And maybe —

That was the most dangerous part of all.

Six months later.

The city stretched wide beneath the pale light of dawn, a cold breeze cutting through the early morning haze. A thin layer of fog curled along the edge of the river, soft and gray against the glow of the rising sun.

Arjun stood at the edge of the rooftop, his hands tucked into the pockets of his dark coat.

His gaze drifted over the city skyline — the jagged spires of glass and steel cutting upward into the pale light. His breath fogged faintly in the cool air.

The ache was still there — low and constant beneath his ribs. A quiet, dull throb that never quite left.

But it was easier now.

Most days.

He had learned to function beneath the weight of it — the emptiness she had left him with.

The hollow stretch of quiet that filled the spaces where she used to be.

It was strange how the pain could become familiar after a while.

Expected.

Almost comforting.

His eyes darkened as his gaze slid toward the street below. Cars passed beneath the early morning light. Pedestrians hurried across the intersections, their collars drawn tight against the cold.

Life had moved on without him.

And somehow, he had kept moving too.

Barely.

A quiet sound stirred behind him — the soft click of approaching footsteps against the rooftop gravel.

"You're up early."

Arjun's gaze didn't shift as Rehan came up beside him.

"Couldn't sleep," Arjun said quietly.

Rehan's brow furrowed. His dark eyes studied Arjun's profile beneath the pale morning light.

"You've been saying that for months," Rehan said.

Arjun's mouth curled faintly.

"I guess I'm consistent."

Rehan's gaze sharpened. "You know this isn't sustainable."

Arjun's eyes narrowed slightly.

"What's not?"

"Pretending you're okay."

Arjun's jaw tightened. His gaze drifted toward the river, the cold breeze brushing across his skin.

"I'm not pretending," Arjun said flatly.

Rehan's brow lifted. "You're not doing much of anything."

Arjun's hand curled faintly at his side. His pulse tightened beneath his skin.

"What do you want me to say?" Arjun said darkly. "That I'm fine? That I'm over it?"

Rehan's mouth tightened.

"You don't have to be over it," Rehan said. "But you can't let her keep controlling you."

Arjun's gaze sharpened. His chest tightened beneath the weight of it.

"She's not controlling me," Arjun said coldly.

Rehan's gaze didn't waver.

"You sure about that?"

Arjun's jaw locked. His hand slid toward the edge of his jacket, his fingers curling loosely over the worn fabric.

"She's gone," Arjun said quietly.

"And yet you still hear her voice, don't you?"

Arjun's chest constricted painfully.

He didn't answer.

He didn't have to.

Rehan's gaze softened slightly.

"You can't stay in this place forever," Rehan said. "She's not coming back."

Arjun's breath scraped low in his throat. His eyes burned faintly beneath the pale light.

"I know," Arjun whispered.

And that was the worst part of it.

She wasn't coming back.

But she was everywhere.

In the shadows. In the quiet. In the sharp twist of his breath when he woke in the dark and thought — for just a second — that he could still feel her there.

He had tried to bury it. To forget her.

But it was like trying to outrun his own shadow.

Rehan's hand clapped gently over his shoulder.

"You have to let her go," Rehan said softly.

Arjun's eyes darkened. His chest squeezed painfully.

"I don't know how," Arjun admitted quietly.

Rehan's gaze sharpened.

"Then maybe it's time to figure it out."

Arjun's breath steadied. His eyes drifted toward the city beyond the edge of the rooftop.

Let her go.

That was what everyone kept telling him.

But no one seemed to understand —

She had *taken* pieces of him when she left.

And now — there was nothing left to rebuild.

Rehan's hand slipped away from his shoulder.

"Take the first step," Rehan said quietly. "Even if it's small."

Arjun's gaze remained fixed on the skyline.

For a long time, neither of them spoke.

And then —

Rehan's phone buzzed faintly. He glanced at it, his brow furrowing.

"I have to go," Rehan said. His gaze lingered on Arjun. "You'll be okay?"

Arjun didn't answer.

Rehan sighed and clapped his shoulder once before turning toward the stairwell.

Arjun stayed where he was, his breath steady beneath the thin bite of the cold. His eyes followed the dark edge of the horizon, the pale light cutting through the fog.

He slid his hands into his pockets, his jaw tightening beneath the quiet weight of it.

Let her go.

He didn't know if he could.

But maybe —

He could learn how to stop holding on.

The city below began to brighten beneath the early morning light.

Arjun's breath sharpened as he closed his eyes.

And for the first time in months —

He let himself breathe.

www.ingramcontent.com/pod-product-compliance
Lightning Source LLC
LaVergne TN
LVHW061614070526
838199LV00078B/7276